MW00585555

THE SIGN ABOVE THE DOOR

Also by WILLIAM W. CANFIELD

Legends of the Iroquois (1902)

The Spotter: A Romance of the Oil Region (1907)

Along the Way (1909)

The White Seneca (1911)

At Seneca Castle (1912)

with J. E. CLARK

Things Worth Knowing about Oneida County (1909)

THE
SIGN ABOVE THE DOOR

BY

 WILLIAM W. CANFIELD

Salem Ridge Press
Emmaus, Pennsylvania

Originally published
1912
The Jewish Publication Society of America

Republished 2006
Salem Ridge Press LLC
4263 Salem Drive
Emmaus, Pennsylvania 18049

www.SalemRidgePress.com

Cover Illustration © 2006 Abigail Mills

ISBN-10: 0-9776786-2-8
ISBN-13: 978-0-9776786-2-4

CONTENTS

PUBLISHER'S NOTE

The Sign Above the Door is exciting historical fiction set at the time of the Exodus of the Hebrews out of Egypt. Rather than simply retelling the Bible story, William Canfield presents a compelling tale that takes place in parallel to the Biblical story. This provides the reader with a greater understanding of the people and culture of the time while remaining faithful to the original account.

As in his other books, William Canfield also presents the reader with many excellent examples of positive character qualities such as loyalty and self-sacrifice as well as underscoring the importance of protecting the honor of women.

In republishing this book, the spelling has been updated and a few very minor changes have been made to the text.

One interesting note is that the Hebrew name of the main female character, Elisheba (אֱלִישֶׁבַע), is composed of two parts, "El" meaning God and "sheba" meaning covenant, making the literal meaning of her name "God is her covenant."

Daniel Mills

February, 2006.

Hieroglyphic Symbols
In order of use

|	1		Man
	10		Pintail Duck
	Battle-axe		Head in profile
	Crown of Egypt	＊	Star
	Woman		Enemy
	Lotus flower		Cobra
	Harp		Cartouche
	(unknown)		Mummy
	Door		Jar
	Reeds		Scimitar
	To sail		Sunshine
	Rowing		Cloth on a pole
	Boat		Water
	Pillars		Hawk

THE SIGN ABOVE THE DOOR

"And Moses called for all the elders of Israel, and said unto them, Draw out and take for yourselves lambs according to your families, and kill the passover sacrifice.

"And ye shall take a bunch of hyssop, and dip in the blood that is in the basin, and strike the lintel and the two side-posts with the blood that is in the basin; and none of you shall go out from the door of his house until the morning.

"And the Lord will pass through to smite the Egyptians; and when he seeth the blood upon the lintel, and on the two side-posts, the Lord will pass over the door, and will not suffer the destroyer to come in unto your houses to smite.

"And ye shall observe this thing, as an ordinance for thee and thy sons forever."

THE
SIGN ABOVE THE DOOR

|

CHAPTER I

MASTER AND MAN

MARTIESEN the adon had dismissed his attendants for the night, and, accompanied only by Peshala, his chief scribe or secretary, awaited the return of his lieutenant from Rameses. Martiesen was one of the most opulent Egyptian governors. He was in command of the Nome of the Prince, considered the most prosperous division in Lower Egypt, in which his family had long enjoyed preferment. Its system of canals had been brought to a state of perfection that insured a sufficient supply of water for the irrigation of the gardens at all times, and the harvests that came from its fields were noted for their abundance and uniform excellence. This nome, or political division, lay upon the eastern bank of the Nile; and embraced not only the land of Goshen, in which dwelt the Israelitish serfs, but also several populous towns and cities, which had been brought to an advanced condition of prosperity during the reign of Rameses II, the last preceding monarch. Close upon its southern border was located the city of Rameses, in which stood the palace of Meneptah, the Pharaoh, or king, of Egypt, who was devoting the energies of his kingdom to the construction of monuments and public works of considerable magnitude.

The ancestral home of the adon was one of beautiful luxury. It stood near the Nile, that mysterious and wonderful river, which has been a highway and source of wealth for untold thousands of years, and about it clustered the dwellings of the officers, superintendents, workmen, and slaves who were required to administer and conduct the affairs of a villa of such importance. In the house were displayed evidences of that Egyptian art which is still the marvel of the world, and to them had been added many rich and curious trophies won in the successful expeditions in which the adon and his ancestors had participated with the victorious armies of a nation which at that time ruled and exacted tribute, not only from the barbarous tribes of Ethiopia, but from Libya, Syria, and the

Phoenicians. Handsome ebony chairs and fauteuils inlaid with ivory, low seats or divans, rich couches, soft mats and rugs, hangings of delicate texture and brilliant colorings interlaced with threads of gold, and cushions of down covered with the finest linen, were displayed in the salon in profusion. Upon tables set apart for this purpose stood jars of sweet ointments, myrrh, frankincense, and choice odors in various forms, brought from Ethiopia, Syria, and Arabia. The ceiling was decorated with an exquisite pattern of lotus flowers upon a background of dark bronze, displaying refined taste and skillful execution. Above the entrance glistened the golden form of the sacred scarab. Curiously shaped instruments of bronze, ivory, and wood, designed for use in war, each no doubt possessing a story of some hard-fought battle, decorated the walls. About them, in singular contrast, were groups of delicate musical instruments, and articles of feminine adornment, probably swept into the baskets of looting soldiers from the rooms of women in whose veins ran royal blood.

The adon, half reclining in a broad chair of fine workmanship, over which was thrown the glistening skin of a leopard, was minutely examining a roll of papyrus that had been placed in his hands by his secretary. Martiesen the adon, scarcely more than twenty-five years of age, was tall, well-formed, and fine-fibered. His countenance bore marks of intellectual cultivation not common to men of that time who devoted themselves either to warfare or to public life, and, from the fact that he read the papyrus with ease, it was apparent that the adon was a scholar as well as a soldier and governor. There was about him that air of firmness which distinguishes the true leader, and it was evident that under his quiet and reserved manner slept both strength and passion, either of which might prove dangerous if provoked. Occasionally, as he perused the text, Martiesen drew the attention of his secretary to omissions or errors, and from the kindly way in which he pointed out the desired corrections, one might argue that he was at once frank and forgiving, for his criticisms were generally in the line of suggestion.

Peshala, the secretary, was of larger frame, but he was not so closely knit as the master, and did not bear the same evidence of force. Upon his face avarice, cunning, and jealousy were blended, with none, however, so marked as to conceal a certain dignified beauty and regularity of features, which enabled him to mask his feelings

when he desired. While his master was bent over
the papyrus, the secretary's eyes wandered about
the luxurious room, occasionally resting with a
hungry, covetous glitter upon some costly ornament set with precious stones, from which the
soft lights in the apartment broke back in
sparkling rays. Then he would covertly glance at
his chief, and over his face would spread a cloud
of such malevolent hate that the man for the
instant was metamorphosed, and was more the
beast than the human being. But when the adon
turned, and with a smile requested alterations in
the record, Peshala, with an obsequious bow,
caught up his stylus, and with apparent cheer-
fulness complied with the request. Once the adon
raised his eyes and discovered the secretary
bending forward and examining the sheath of a
dagger lying with other curios in a niche near
him. The sheath was set with gems in great
profusion, and was alone worth the ransom of a
king.

"What is it, Peshala?" asked the adon, quietly.
"Have you not seen the dagger of the Libyan
prince often enough for it no longer to excite
your curiosity to such an extent as to make you
unheedful of what is passing? Or were you thinking that you would be pleased to call the weapon

your own?"

"No, my lord adon, it is not that," replied the secretary, quickly recovering himself. "My thoughts turned to the warrior who possessed the weapon before it came into your hands. He was my countryman."

"Yes, I remember that you are a Libyan by birth. But you came to Egypt when scarcely more than a boy, and have been taught all her ways. You can have little love for the arid plains and barren mountains of Libya, which you can scarcely be able to recall with accuracy or pleasure."

Peshala shook his head doubtfully. "Often I dream of those plains and mountains," he said, "but more frequently of the brave men who were swept down by the hosts of Egypt, and lost their lives and treasure."

"Aye, war has ever its rugged edge," said the adon, "and had we not repelled the Libyans, they would have devastated Egypt. As for this dagger, it was taken in honorable battle. I was but a youth when we fought to stay the Libyan invasion, and while the battle waged, I came in contact with a powerful warrior many years my senior. When his chariot bore down upon me, he laughed in derision, as though he considered the contest beneath his caste. I so guided my chargers that the wheels of our chariots were locked, and the Libyan, still disdaining my youth, struck carelessly at me with his sword. I parried successfully, and his weapon flew from his hand, and then, before he could seize his spear, I leaped upon his chariot and struck, with my battle-axe, a blow that cleft his skull. As was my right in battle, I took from the Libyan his weapons, of which this dagger was the most curious and valuable. From its appearance I believe it was an heirloom in the family of the man who carried it, and as it was my first trophy in war, I prize it highly."

The adon stepped forward, and raised the dagger from its resting-place. "Look," he said as he drew the blade from its scabbard, "in all Egypt there is not its equal."

The weapon was of superior workmanship, and its hardened and tempered bronze blade, polished like a mirror, was so skillfully wrought that it possessed the pliability of steel. The handle was inlaid with silver and gold, interlaced to form curious figures. The sheath, also of bronze, bore many jewels, several of them of unusual size. As the adon displayed the beautiful object, and drew attention to its perfect shape and workmanship, Peshala could scarcely control his emotion. The adon was so intent upon the weapon that he did not observe that his secretary was on the point of springing upon him. The man's eyes contracted, until they were mere points glittering like an angry reptile's, and each instant he crouched lower, like a cat about to leap upon its prey. It was fortunate that the intensity of the situation was at this moment broken by a musical peal from the bars of metal hanging in the portico, announcing the arrival of a guest.

"It is Panas," said the adon as he sheathed the dagger, and replaced it in the niche. "Hasten to admit him."

Peshala hesitated an instant, as a man who has heard, but does not comprehend, and then he started, with unsteady steps, to obey the command; but not until he crossed the salon, and entered the hall leading to the portico, did he regain his composure. Martiesen noted this with curiosity. He knew little concerning the scribe, who had come to him about three months before, bearing recommendations as to equipment for his duties. The adon found him ready, active, and intelligent, but given somewhat to moody silence. Previously he had never shown unusual emotion in the presence of his master, and its display at this time was the source of some surprise. Before

Martiesen satisfied himself as to the cause, the hangings parted, and Panas, followed by Peshala, entered the salon.

"Ah, Panas, your return is welcome; we have awaited your coming since sunset. But I know that the delay was not of your own choice, for tardiness never has been charged against you."

"No, my lord adon," replied the lieutenant, as he advanced and accepted the invitation to be seated. "The delay was unavoidable, for the home journey was taken up immediately after the completion of my mission."

"Of this I have no doubt, Panas, for I am sure you do not especially love the city of our august ruler. But tell me, did you obtain audience with the king?"

"I did not, my lord. The Pharaoh was engaged in the consideration of some plans, in company with the royal architects, and would not permit interruption. I was content, therefore, to lodge your petition in the hands of the ab, who in turn brought it to the attention of Meneptah, when he laid aside the plans and partook of refreshment."

"And is there a reply?"

"Yes. The king was angered at what he termed your insistence, and, calling his scribe, he dictated his commands."

The lieutenant presented a packet covered with soft, flexible leather, wrapped with three narrow strips of linen, each sealed with the cartouche of the Pharaoh. Martiesen received the packet with due reverence, and, placing it upon a table, authorized his secretary to break the seals. Peshala performed this task with exquisite care. He severed the bands of linen so skillfully that the wax which bore the cartouche was not marred. From the wrappings he drew a papyrus roll, and awaited further commands.

"Read," said the adon, "and the words written at the command of the Pharaoh shall be obeyed."

Slowly unrolling the papyrus and speaking as the hieroglyphics came to view, Peshala read:

"Meneptah, Ruler of Lower and Upper Egypt and Wearer of two crowns, Lord and Pharaoh over all this land and of the People within its borders, doth command Martiesen, son of Peturis, Adon and Governor of the Nome of the Prince, and Captain of the Officers and Soldiers of the Pharaoh who have in charge the Hebrew People:

"That he shall not remit one jot or tittle of the

Tasks which have, in the judgment of the King, been placed upon the Hebrews — But shall require of them all that hath been commanded, that they may not waste their Days in Idleness, seeking to stir up Insurrection and Sedition against the Kingdom in which they are held as Slaves — That it is the Will of Meneptah that there be no relaxation of their Work — That the tale of Bricks required of each male Hebrew will not be diminished, lest the workmen of the King in the Treasure-Cities and upon the Monuments which are being built to the Glory of Egypt may have no materials with which to build — And if it be true, what thou sayest by the hand of Panas, that the women of the Hebrews and their children go forth to gather stubble in the fields and sedge in the Canals that the men may complete their work — Then so be it.

Meneptah.

"Executed and confirmed by Erieus the son of Phaures, Ab of Meneptah — Pharaoh of all Egypt — Gods of the Beneficent Gods, of the Father-Loving Gods, of the Paternal Gods, and of the Mother-Loving Gods — Amen."

Silence rested upon the three for a moment

after the secretary ceased to read. Then the adon spoke:

"In the name of the Pharaoh these commands must be executed, even though Egypt suffer. Peshala, see that the couriers are summoned to report to me at dawn. And you, Panas, seek rest, that you may come in the morning to the court, and there tell me what new rumors you have heard at Rameses."

The adon and his lieutenant left the apartment, and the secretary, still holding the papyrus in his hands, remained beside the table, until he heard their footsteps cross the court. Then he rolled the papyrus carefully, and restored it to its covering. The linen bands with their unbroken seals were wrapped in a square of silk, and this was deposited in a small casket containing papyrus, stylus, writing-fluids, and wax. Almost noiselessly the man moved about the salon, extinguishing the lamps and tapers, until the room was illumined only by the rays of the moon, which came gently through the opalescent windows. Carefully he crept towards the niche in which reposed the Libyan weapon. His slender fingers lightly passed over the wall, until his hand came to the resting-place of the blade, and then he seized upon it as a prize, and held it against his breast.

"My father's dagger," he whispered, in a voice choking with emotion. "How well I knew there was not in all this world its fellow, and that this which I have found here, and have sought throughout all Egypt, must have been his. To-night, when the murderer boasted how he robbed Libya of her noblest prince, my quest came to an end. Here is the man upon whom I will wreak vengeance — and I, the son, stood by and heard his idle tale, and did not strike him dead, though every muscle in my body throbbed with the desire! But when my arm would strike, I thought that a death that comes so quickly would be no punishment, and so I stayed the blow."

He stood a moment in silence, with uplifted face, and then he spoke again:

"It was not a truthful tale he told, for neither one, nor two, nor three such as this Egyptian could bring the Prince of Libya to his death. It was told my mother that her husband was surrounded by a score of hired soldiers, who overcame him with spears, and the master of the murderous band plundered his corpse. Yet this Martiesen boasts that he, a boy, won the vantage in fair and single-handed contest — and makes the boast to one who knows the claim is false! So I will pull him down, and tread into the dust his power and insolence, and grind his pride under my feet, until he begs his gods to send him death and thus relief."

The impassioned man swayed from side to side as he held the weapon to his breast, clinging to it with the eagerness and love a mother would shower upon a child from whom she had been long parted. Tenderly he brought it to his lips, and from a great ruby in the handle the pale moonlight was reflected over his face like the scarlet glow of blood. He stood a moment thus, and then tremblingly replaced the venerated heirloom within the niche.

With bowed head and shaking limbs he crept backward to the entrance.

II

CHAPTER II

THE AWAKENING

THE season of the waters had passed, and the husbandmen of all the land were diligently employed with their tasks. Everywhere the fertile soil, which for months is held each year in the grasp of the Nile, was being tilled and planted. Men and women went early to the fields, and from bags of matting they threw, in rows or broadcast, the seed of wheat, barley, rye, sorghum, and many vegetables, upon the quickening earth. Then other women or children came, with droves of cattle, goats, or asses, which trampled the seed into the soft ground. In Goshen, the section set apart for the Hebrews, the labor of planting fell most heavily upon the women and the children, for the king exacted that each male above the age of fourteen years should make a certain tale of bricks daily, for the building of his treasure-cities and monuments. Taskmasters were appointed to see that the Hebrews performed these duties, and the burden was enforced with a heavy hand.

There came among the Hebrews at this time two aged men of their own blood, grave, sedate, serious men, who bore upon their countenances that impress of responsibility which comes with a tremendous task fully realized and understood even in contemplation. Within a few days after their arrival, a strange assembly was brought together. The elders of the tribes were summoned, and they were told by the men who had appeared from the desert, that the God who had guided their fathers to this land four centuries before was now determined to bring them out of their bondage, and thus keep the covenant made with their progenitor.

There remained among the Hebrews scarcely a trace of their ancient religion. Generations had passed since they had been taught by their own priests. They were in constant touch with those who held beasts and reptiles sacred and sacrificed to Isis, Osiris, Nub, Anpu, Kadesh, and Apisi. Only faint traditions remained of that Being in

whom Joseph had abiding faith, nor was He
known under His distinct appellation. With
burning words and wondrous signs, Moses and
his brother Aaron pressed their mission upon
their hearers, and awakened them to the
knowledge that there was a Champion who had
heard their murmurings, and witnessed their
afflictions, and who would bring them forth from
their sorrows. Then the Hebrew fathers bowed
their heads, and worshipped God.

At length a plan was formed, and the two went
to the city of Rameses, and sought audience with
the Pharaoh. They told the king that the God of
the Hebrews had commanded their people to go
into the wilderness to worship; but the king
questioned an authority that set itself up as
greater than that of the Pharaoh, and demanded
by what right they presumed to call the people
from their work. If the Hebrews were thought to
have leisure for a journey of three days into the
wilderness, it must be that their burdens were not
so heavy as represented; and he forthwith gave
orders that hereafter straw should not be
provided with which to make the bricks, though
no part of the required number should be
remitted.

Then came many weary days, for the wives and daughters, the old men and women, the sick, the maimed, and the feeble of the Hebrews must needs go out into the fields and along the canals through which the water was let in upon the lands, everywhere seeking straw and stubble, and papyrus branches and sedge, that the men might complete their tasks, and escape the beatings at the hands of the masters set over them. It was not unnatural that deep murmurs arose from the oppressed people, or that they looked with sorrow upon the day in which they had committed their cause into the hands of unknown adventurers.

One day in the middle of the season of vegetation, there went out a strange visitation over Egypt. In the morning, as Meneptah came, with his retinue, to the river to bathe, the Hebrew prophets stood before him, and declared that unless the request be granted, and their people permitted to depart upon their pilgrimage to worship, the waters of Egypt would turn to blood. The king with his counsellors and magicians laughed at the improbability of such an event's happening, whereupon Aaron reached forth and smote the waters of the Nile with a rod, and, waving his hands toward the four parts of the earth, uttered words which he had been commanded to speak.

Behold! before the very eyes of the king and his servants, the sparkling waters of the Nile grew sluggish in their course, and became as blood! And in the river, the pools, the ponds, the canals, and reservoirs, wherever the Egyptians sought water for seven days, they found none that was not rendered unfit for their use by the blight invoked by the fearful messengers from the Hebrew God.

In the weeks that followed, there fell upon the land a succession of calamities. Myriads of frogs came croaking from the waters, and occupied every space; lice and flies, as numerous as the grains of sand in the desert, covered the ground, or darkened the air. A distemper affected the beasts; boils and blains broke out upon mankind. Then the prophet brought down the vengeance of Heaven in lightning, thunder, and hail, such as no man in that country had beheld previously. Following soon, came a flight of locusts, which destroyed much of the wheat, the rye, and the growing crops.

Vainly the priests, some of the princes, and the

king himself attempted to explain away these phenomena as arising from natural causes, but they could not satisfy the people, and there spread abroad a deep-seated belief that this unknown God who was fighting the battles of the Hebrews was more powerful than the gods of the Egyptians, and discontent was expressed, because the king did not take measures to appease the wrath which threatened the destruction of the country and its inhabitants.

It was at this time that Martiesen was emboldened to dispatch, by the hand of Panas, a letter to the king, following mild protests previously made, in which he asked that the laws against the Hebrews be modified, and suggested that by this means further punishment might be averted. The answer to the letter was disappointing. The adon expected that the king would take into consideration his governor's experience with the Hebrews, and his intimate knowledge of their characteristics, and would be guided by his suggestions. Therefore, when the adon met Panas on the morning following the lieutenant's return from Rameses, bearing the king's sharp order that every requirement be enforced, he made no effort to conceal his fear that further oppression would result in more serious consequences than any heretofore encountered.

"You may speak freely upon all you have learned at the palace, Panas. It will assist in determining my course," said the adon.

They were in the open conservatory of the court, partaking of figs, dates, rice cakes, and melons. Before the lieutenant replied, he arose and walked behind the screen of plants against which they were seated, examining with care those places in the deep foliage in which one might easily rest without detection from the court.

"What I have to tell, my lord," said Panas, resuming his seat on the spacious settle, "comes from Portis the scribe. He disclosed, with many injunctions of secrecy, except as to yourself, that of the thirty judges twenty and three have petitioned the king to bid the Hebrews depart with all their holdings. Many princes of the blood have joined in the petitions, and among them he mentioned Phibis of Giheza and Peteartres of Thebes, as well as others of equal rank. But the priests and magicians have prevailed on the Pharaoh to turn a deaf ear to this counsel, and they keep him occupied with poems and addresses, in which it is declared, with oft-repeated words of praise, that he is the most powerful of all the rulers in the world, that his armies are invincible, and the God of the Hebrews cannot prevail against him. Erieus the ab has united with the priests and magicians, and is constantly urging the king to seize and imprison the Hebrew prophets, or to send an army against the Hebrews themselves, putting to death all the males, or sending them captive to the quarries at Syene. He purposes to divide their cattle among the temples and convert what treasure they may have to the use of the Pharaoh."

"And did Portis say how the king regards this counsel?"

"He says that he looks upon it with favor, and is almost upon the point of summoning his captains to arrange a campaign of this nature."

"Monstrous!" declared the adon. "The plan is not only dangerous to our country, but cruel in the extreme. Have the judges and princes expressed themselves upon this suggestion of the ab?"

"They have, my lord, and in doing so have warned the king that if such a course is taken, he may expect to see it result in the ruin of his country, if not its utter annihilation. They do not shut their eyes to the fact that the Hebrew God has control of all the natural elements."

The lieutenant paused and glanced carefully about the court. Then he leaned forward until his lips were but a short distance from the adon's face. "My lord; Portis declared that this plan of the Pharaoh is so disturbing to certain of the judges and princes that they have been consulting privately as to means to prevent it."

"What means, Panas, may be employed against the will of the Pharaoh, whose nod or slightest wish, or whose beck or call is law itself?"

"There is one way, my lord adon, and it is not new in Egypt."

"And that is, Panas?"

"The usurpation of the crown!"

The adon started as though he had been dealt a blow. For a moment he looked into his lieutenant's face in speechless astonishment, and it was not until he had made several attempts to speak that he found his tongue.

"Usurpation! Why, Panas, the very thought is dangerous! It would lead to untold slaughter and destruction, with all the horrors attendant upon civil war. I cannot believe that the intention is serious."

"Indeed it is, my lord."

"Upon whom do the complotters purpose to bestow the uraeus, should they succeed?"

The eyes of the lieutenant did not waver from the face of his chief as he arose and bowed, as though already doing homage to a Pharaoh. "Upon Martiesen the adon, firstborn and only son of Peturia, a prince of the royal blood through his mother, a daughter of a Pharaoh," he said impressively.

The adon leaped to his feet in excitement and walked rapidly up and down the conservatory. Twice he paused to scan the face of Panas, as though seeking to discover either concealment or treachery; but the young officer returned the scrutiny with open frankness that assured his superior that he did not harbor deceit.

"Panas, this cannot be," he said with determination. "Among the ancestors of Martiesen there has been no traitor to the king."

"Aye, my lord, this is well known to me. But until Meneptah came to the throne, there had been, in four centuries, no king in whose reign the danger to our country was so great."

"The provocation that justifies the revolt of a people against their ruler must be deep indeed, for civil strife carries with it more direful consequences than any form of war," declared Martiesen. "All efforts to change the policy of the Pharaoh have not been exhausted, and until every means has been put forth to bring the king to a realization of the true state, we must think of neither revolt nor usurpation."

"My lord, in the early evening a number of the princes will come to the villa. They will make the journey upon the pretext of a pilgrimage for pleasure, but in truth to gain an opportunity of laying their plans before you. These I do not know, but only this, that the complotters have taken no rash steps. The ancient law, long regarded as necessary to the well-being of the state, furnishes abundant reason for declaring the throne of Egypt vacant, and placing thereupon one in whom the thirty judges may agree are vested those qualities which go to make a wise and prudent ruler. It is recognized, my lord, that you have the confidence of the leaders in the Hebrew settlements, for your treatment of this people, so far as it has been possible for you to temper the commands of the king, has been wise and humane. It is argued that if you will consent to the revolt, the Hebrews would join you, and thus bring no inconsiderable force to the enterprise."

"Ah, the poor Hebrews! Why, Panas, they know nothing of war, and at best could be little more than an unorganized mob of slaves. I do not doubt that in this nation there sleep qualities that make great warriors and wise statesmen; but these slumbering attributes have not been developed, and those who think they could organize, among this downtrodden people, companies that would meet and withstand chariots of the king, know little of the conditions."

"But, my lord, could not some help be secured of the Hebrew God through the wonderworker, Moses?"

"I am convinced that Moses of himself, though possessing a strong personality, has no power. There is something more to this God of the Hebrews, whom Moses obeys, than to those gods whom we have been taught to reverence. You and I, who have had such intimate relations with the Hebrews, are satisfied that this is true, and though we bow at the shrine of Isis and Osiris, it is with the knowledge that such devotion has no virtue. If the God of the Hebrews has determined upon the liberation of His people, then no power the Pharaoh may put forth can prevent the consummation of that plan; nor is it probable that the seizure of the government by others would operate as a stay to the course this mysterious Being has chosen to follow."

"True, my lord, I believe it is as you say. However, I trust you will meet the messengers, who will place before you, much better than I can hope to do, the urgent reasons for action."

"Indeed, Panas, I will meet them as becomes their rank, for it is ever a pleasure to discuss with learned men the matters that appertain to the state. We may hit upon some plan by which the tyranny of the king may be modified. Meneptah has grown cruel with advancing years; he no longer grasps the reins with gentle force, but leaves everything to the priests. It is possible that the nobles, recognizing this, may decide to demand a regency, for surely the Pharaoh is in his dotage."

"He was an old man when he came to the throne, my lord."

"Yes, and it was at a time when a younger man was sorely needed in Egypt."

"If a younger man was needed then, how much greater is the need at this hour."

"Ah, Panas," said the adon, laughing, "I see that you are ever a soldier, and I am almost persuaded that you are anxious for war. It was my hope that the beautiful Serah would turn your thoughts into other channels."

"My thoughts, my lord, are first for my country and second for you, whom I serve."

"I grant that, Panas," said the adon, approaching and placing his arm about the lieutenant's shoulders, "but I should not blame you if they were sometimes first for Serah, for her beauty and manner are most bewitching. But come, further discussion may wait. Let us give orders for the preparation of a festival that will do honor to our coming guests. The time is short, and we must not delay if we would make the welcome meet and proper."

CHAPTER III

ELISHEBA

THE fauteuil upon which Martiesen and Panas were seated was a somewhat heavy piece of furniture, with carved ebony skirting along the front and with ends that came to the floor. At the back, the skirting was not so deep, and a space of nearly two handbreadths remained between the ornamentation and the pavement. Under this seat Peshala had concealed himself before the adon and lieutenant entered the court. The secretary scented a secret which he desired to possess, and he was quite sure that, when the two talked together concerning the lieutenant's visit to Rameses, it would develop. He realized that there was danger in playing the eavesdropper, but when men enter a game in which the stakes are high, they do not hesitate at the danger point, but laugh at prudence, and leap forward with one absorbing thought uppermost.

When Martiesen and Panas had disappeared, Peshala carefully tilted the heavy seat forward, until he could crawl from his hiding-place. Glancing quickly around to discover if he had been observed, the man arranged his clothing leisurely, and brushed the litter and dust from his tunic. Then, bringing a chair to the table, the Libyan opened his portfolio, and began to write rapidly.

"A point, my fine adon," he said half-aloud, "and Peshala the scribe will set it down, that when he appears before the king no word may be forgotten."

His stylus traced the paper with quick, nervous dashes for a few moments, and then he spoke again: "A conspiracy, born in Rameses and to be fed and nurtured here tonight, when the other traitors arrive! It is more advantageous to my purpose than I dared hope for. Ah, but how cunningly he played the dullard to Panas, and made him think that he, the noble adon, was true to the Pharaoh, and would not consent to lead a revolt. Poor fool! Could I not read in his voice how he thirsted for power? And yet, to further his ends and make others the readier to give him aid, he pretended to put the crown aside, and prated of his loyalty — and Panas believed! Will Meneptah believe — will Erieus the ab believe that Martiesen is white and clean as linen, when I lay this evidence before them? What said he of the Pharaoh? Ah, yes, that he was in his dotage; and Panas agreed. I can see the king now, and hear him roar when I read him this. In his dotage! Thus spake Martiesen, I will say, 'Meneptah has grown cruel with advancing years; he no longer grasps the reins with gentle force, but leaves everything to the priests. It is possible that the nobles may decide to demand a regency, for surely the Pharaoh is in his dotage.' Then will the palace tremble, and I shall hear the order to bring the adon before the throne on which he sits who has held his mighty power all these years by the sway of a scepter that has never faltered when directed against one who for an instant questioned his authority."

He arose from the table, and clasped his hands with intensity, and laughed as only such a man, or an evil spirit, can laugh — not with mirth and happiness, but with the mumbling sounds of one who gloats. Again he resumed his writing, but in another moment he started to his feet.

"Tonight! Ah, the conspirators come hither,

and will feast while they conclude their plot! Then, in the morning, they will sleep — hours — for there will be wine and an abundance of food. They will not leave here until near the evening of tomorrow. Surprise — surprise! I shall go to Rameses as they feast, and while they are sleeping, the force may be brought here to apprehend the plotters upon the grave charge of conspiracy. And I, Peshala the Libyan, shall be there when they come as prisoners — there to witness their downfall — his downfall — and receive my reward."

He heard footsteps, and, as he rolled the papyrus, a slave ushered a woman into the retreat. Peshala advanced, and bowed with dignity to the veiled form. "In the absence of my lord, the adon," he said, "I am fortunate to welcome the daughter of Darda to the villa."

"The errand upon which I came is for my father and with the adon, whom I should be pleased to see at once," replied the woman, in a clear and musical voice.

"My lord is this moment engaged in issuing orders for a festival which he is to give this evening, but I will soon inform him of your presence."

With a wave of his hand Peshala dismissed the

slave, and then turned to the girl, who ignored the proffered chair, and remained standing. The loose robe of linen in which she was clad draped a tall, lithe form of beautifully molded pro-portions. There was a symmetry and poise about her which stamped her as of more than ordinary clay. Her face, half-veiled, as was the custom of those who rode in unshaded boats upon the Nile, gave promise of a beauty that would command attention even in that land of beautiful women. Her eyes were of that deep and lustrous black which carry nothing of the cruel, but rather melting compassion and earnest sympathy. And yet, as one looked into their quiet depths, there were to be discerned slumbering resources, awaiting only the call for action to bring them into play.

"I am most fortunate today," said Peshala, when they were alone, "but the greatest favor that has yet fallen to me is being present to receive Elisheba, the fairest of all the Hebrew maidens, for I have something of importance to say to her."

The girl's eyes brightened, and she took a step forward. "Has the Pharaoh granted the prayer of the adon?" she asked.

"My lady, your question must remain for the adon to answer," replied the secretary, with caution. "What I have to say more nearly concerns yourself — yes, and the members of your family."

"Nothing can more nearly concern us than that which relates to all the Hebrew people," she replied.

Peshala threw off all reserve, for he feared interruption at any moment, and he wished to push his advantage. "It must have been heard by the wise Darda, and by the daughter to whom he gives every confidence, that the Pharaoh has the extinction of the Hebrew race in his mind."

He paused and watched her eyes for some token to assure him that she knew of this design, but she gave no recognition.

"The king has long feared their growing power, and the priests have let pass no opportunity of adding to his concern. Recently, as I have heard, he has taken counsel with those who remain about his court upon a plan to put the Hebrews to the sword, and at any moment a decree to this effect may be issued. Fortunately, there has come to me occasion to do the king great service, and when it is rendered, I may ask of him what I will, and it will be granted."

A swift, half-alarmed glance about her was Elisheba's only answer.

"The Pharaoh is never unmindful of those who are true to him," he continued, "nor does he neglect to punish his enemies. For that which I shall disclose to Meneptah, the Libyan scribe will be made rich and powerful, and in his hands will be placed authority which even princes of the blood have vainly striven years to attain."

"All this is nothing to me, Peshala. Why do you tell it?" she asked.

"It can be made of as much importance to you, Elisheba, as it is to me," he replied. "For, think you if I then ask the king to separate Darda, the Hebrew, and his daughters, from their people, and give them over into my charge, that he will refuse?"

She flinched at his question, and he saw alarm in her eyes.

"I possess a secret of such import that its disclosure may hold his throne for the Pharaoh — and this I shall carry to his ears before the sun rises tomorrow. The gratitude of Meneptah will lead him to give what I ask," he declared, as he came to her side, and made an attempt to take her hand. But Elisheba moved quickly away from him, and looked with anxiety toward the entrance. In a moment his frown gave place to a smile, and he simulated tender passion.

"Elisheba, I am a Libyan in whose veins is the blood of one of the noblest men, a prince in his own country. But I became a servant to the Egyptians for a purpose that is now nearly fulfilled. In all my years in Egypt I have not swerved from that purpose, nor did there enter one tender thought in my heart until I saw you — a Hebrew in bondage with your people. Then to my design was added the resolution that you should share my triumph. The hour for the realization of my dreams and that for which I have striven are but a day distant. The opportunity of sharing my victory is in your hand."

The girl made a gesture of protest. "This cannot be, Peshala. I am of the Hebrews, in bondage, as you taunt me. So I will remain, even though it be for a slaughter at the command of the Egyptian king. But of this I have no fear, for there will be stretched forth a hand so powerful that it will pluck my people from every peril, a Power against which even the forces of this monarch cannot prevail."

"Do you mean the Hebrew God?"

She bowed in reply.

"A mere wonderworking trick on the part of a cunning impostor, who will soon reach the limit of his magic, and who is laughed at even now by the wisest in Egypt."

"But the wisest often err."

"Not in exposing such false claims as those made by this Moses, who, having taken advantage of a series of natural calamities, loudly prates that they are the work of a God whom he has conjured up, and who is without form or temple. Banish out of your mind hope for succor from such a source, and choose that which offers certain escape, not only for yourself, but for your younger sisters and aged father."

"It were better to perish," she said firmly.

"Am I, who shall be higher than the adon in power, so odious that you would prefer death to my embrace?"

"Peshala, I have no love for you; but if I had, and you could offer me the diadem of the queen, still I would not turn my back upon my people."

He caught her wrist in a grasp like that of a vise, and, bringing her close to his side, fairly hissed a reply: "I know to whom you have given your love. It is to this Martiesen, and if he should utter one word of invitation, you would desert your father, your people, aye, and your invisible God, and become the adon's slave! You think he loves you, for have I not seen you plume yourself over his soft glances, and bend a willing ear to his words, which ever took on a tenderer tone in your presence? But what love can this Egyptian of noble birth have for you, or for any woman of the Hebrews, when by a wave of his hand he may summon you to his couch? Love! The Egyptians know not its meaning. Living, they are as cold and heartless as the mummies that crowd their tombs, and Martiesen is no exception among his race."

His manner changed, and now he spoke with low intensity: "Elisheba, I will teach you what is love! In my Libyan home you shall take rank with the proudest and best. No hour of the day will I cease to sing of your beauty, and all the brave deeds that have come down to me from long generations of noble ancestors will find vent in that passion that shall link your life with mine."

Peshala sought to draw the frightened and resisting girl to his arms, but with a quick effort Elisheba released herself from his hold, and leaped to the alarm that hung a few paces behind them. Catching the hammer from its resting-place upon the lower bar, she pointed the way to the entrance.

"Go, Peshala, go quickly, and speak no further words, and I will forget what you have said, as coming from one beside himself. But if you do not go, I shall summon aid, and to those who come I shall tell all."

The baffled Libyan, his face dark and scowling with rage, knew that a blow of the hammer upon the metal bars would almost instantly be answered by slaves. Nor did he doubt that the woman who stood before him, and with outstretched hand pointed the way he should go, would hesitate to give the threatened stroke. Slowly he gathered up his papyrus records, and concealed them in his tunic, but his eyes never wavered from the face of the statue-like girl who stood before him. One step he took towards her, and, pausing as he saw the silver hammer trembling for its quick descent, muttered a curse upon her head.

Then Peshala turned and left the retreat.

||||

CHAPTER IV

THE ADON

As Peshala disappeared, Elisheba loosened her veil, and for a moment buried her face in a cluster of lotus flowers, seeking to forget in their beauty and fragrance the unpleasant meeting with one whom she had ever viewed with suspicion and dislike. As she raised her face from the blossoms, her full beauty was betrayed. Her complexion was pure olive, now heightened by a tinge of color brought to the fair cheeks by the excitement through which she had just passed. Her features were regularly and finely cut, displaying strength of character and firmness of purpose that matched well with a fine physical development, and did not overshadow those subtle evidences of modesty which men in all ages have found most attractive among the charms of woman. There was in her bearing nothing of the masculine, and yet it was evident that she possessed tremendous self-reliant force and bravery, which, should occasion demand it, could be depended upon to sustain her in an encounter with death itself, without permitting her to betray cowardice.

She struck the upper bars of the alarm, and the bell-like notes were still quivering through the court when a slave appeared. He was directed to inform his master of her presence. Then she turned again to the luxuriant flowers, and was engaged in the admiration of their beauty, when Martiesen entered.

"I am not only happy to welcome you to the villa, Elisheba," he said, advancing to her side, "but am pleased to see you among my blossoms. The slave this moment informed me that you were waiting, and I came at once, fearing that your presence had been overlooked."

"No, my lord, I but recently arrived, and, not finding you in the salon, came directly to the conservatory, to be with the roses and lotus flowers while awaiting you."

"Their good fortune is to be envied, for the visits of Elisheba to the villa have been rare."

He placed a chair for her at the table, and ordered fruit for her refreshment. "You have a message for me from your father?" he asked.

"Yes, my lord, my father has been most anxious to learn whether the appeal to the Pharaoh has been answered favorably. He desired your pardon for what may appear unseemly haste, but he urged that the danger in delay is great, and so he sent me with two rowers, that he might receive the tidings early."

"Ere this Darda and all the men of Israel have learned the result of the appeal," said the adon, sadly, "for the couriers left at dawn to inform the Hebrews that the Pharaoh will remit no part of the tasks. His commands are here, and it remains for me to execute them."

"Your duty is plain to all, my lord. The Hebrew prophets and elders know that in your heart there is a desire that the bond of slavery be raised from their people; they also know that you may not refuse to do that which the king decrees."

The adon made no reply, and was absorbed a few moments in thought. He was clearly distressed over the situation confronting him, for the further persecution of the Hebrews was contrary to his judgment, and he feared its results.

"Can you tell me where I may find the prophets?" he asked, rousing from his reverie.

"They have retired into Goshen to await the further commands of our God," was her reply.

"And it is said among your people that other plagues will follow?" he inquired.

The girl hesitated, and the adon, noticing this, told her that she might continue to trust him as in the past. He was hopeful of doing something for the welfare of Egypt, and he believed that at this time it could be accomplished only through clemency and kindness to her people. Thus reassured, Elisheba replied to his question.

"The prophets have taught us that this all-powerful God has every force of nature at His command. He not only guides the gentle breeze that kisses our sails upon the Nile but with His breath can overturn the great pyramids, and grind into the dust of the desert the massive stones of which they are built. They teach us further that to those who obey the law of this God, He is loving, tender, kind, and forgiving; but from those who set themselves in opposition to His will, He will strip all pride, even if in so doing He must utterly destroy. You, my lord, have witnessed the wonders this God has wrought in Egypt, and are well aware that what He has demanded has not been surrendered — and yet you ask if other plagues are to follow?"

"I know it was but an idle question, Elisheba. Still, all that which the prophets teach is so mysterious and strange that I am ever wondering and questioning. What I have seen, leads me to believe that the Hebrew God is more powerful than Isis and Osiris. He is the Father of the Nile, for its waters obey Him and turn to blood; He is lord of the air, for He commands, and the tempests appear; He speaks to the sand, and it becomes insects and reptiles. All this have I learned, as He has laid His heavy hand upon my people, and it has filled me with alarm for that which is to come. Nor am I alone in this, for even now princes and nobles are starting on a journey hither, in the hope that by consultation we may devise some plan through which the king may be brought to reason. I trust we may succeed, but the message from your father, that danger rests in delay, increases my anxiety. A few days are necessary to mature our plans, and I bid you charge your father to seek the prophets at once and implore them to withhold, if possible, the hand of their God from further chastisement."

She bowed in obedience to his command, and rose to depart.

"Elisheba, I would not have you return to Zoan, until I have told you what I have asked from your father, and what is nearest to my heart. For many months I have endeavored to remove the obstacles that prevent me from seeking you in marriage. It is an ancient law in Egypt that a prince of the blood may not take a bondwoman as his lawful wife, and though it is true that your lineage runs in a direct line to Joseph, who was a prince in this land, and you are thus my equal in blood, marriage between us would not be lawful until the Pharaoh raises the ban of slavery from your shoulders."

The girl stood modestly before him, the color deepening upon her cheeks, but she made no reply.

"I despair in my effort, for to each request the king returns answer that I am free to take you as my slave, as the law provides, and asks what more I can in reason desire. Should failure attend the plans the princes decide to adopt, I am determined to cast my lot in with the Hebrews, and together we will follow where the prophets lead, for I cannot ask you to become my slave. Nay, it must be so, for your gentle manners and loveliness have so won my heart that even the highest favor of Meneptah can bring no such happiness as I should find by your side."

He gazed into her face with tenderest affection.

"These plans, my lord, will they lead to revolt against the king?"

Martiesen glanced around with a start. "Who has said this to you, Elisheba?"

"No one, my lord. It came to my heart as a fear."

"There are many in Egypt who think this the only course," he replied.

"And do you expect some of them at the villa tonight?" she asked, and he bowed in reply to her question.

"My lord, I beg that you will take no part with them, for the effort will be fruitless, and will only serve to put you in great peril. Even now it is known to one who would betray you that conspiracy is on foot."

"Known, Elisheba!" cried the adon, leaping to his feet. "Speak, girl, what knowledge have you of this? Has a traitor to the princes stood upon the river bank and shouted to those who are passing, or do the people of Zoan read the hearts of men far distant?"

"They do not, my lord. From one of your own household came my knowledge. When I entered the conservatory, Peshala was writing at this table. I requested that you be informed of my presence, but he put me off, and sought to gain favor by boasting that he was in possession of a secret, which he would soon disclose to the Pharaoh, and which would make him rich, powerful, and influential. This secret can be none other than one most nearly concerning you."

Wrath, amazement, perplexity, and finally incredulity passed over the adon's face. "It is impossible, Elisheba, that Peshala should have learned the object of this visit of the princes. All that I know was brought by Panas, who is honor and truth itself. Not one of the slaves was in the court as we talked, and I recall that Panas took the precaution of examining the shrubbery, to see that no one was in hiding. Peshala is a dreamer, and for months has been working at designs, which he expects will yield him great renown as an architect. He claims to have solved an important problem in construction, which will induce the king to place him at the head of some of his extensive works. In veiled language he carried the project to you, adding his boasts, in the hope that you would be dazzled with his dream of wealth and position. He knows nothing of this which is so near the hearts of those who are coming, and he can bring danger to neither the princes nor myself."

"But, my lord, though the secret may have been guarded, I cannot dismiss the fear that in some manner he has learned that of which you speak. I beg you to keep watch upon his movements, and make sure that he learns nothing of what passes between you and your guests."

"I will be cautious. The secretary shall hear only that which may be told with safety to the Pharaoh himself, and if he betrays a sign that stamps him as a traitor, he shall be dealt with as he deserves."

"Before I return, my lord, I should tell you what may guide you in your actions. In a covenant made centuries ago, the God of the Hebrews chose out and set us apart as His peculiar people, destined for the work which He has planned, and from which we cannot escape. As yet we do not know what the work is; we know only our duty to follow where He points the way. The message has come that, once we are released from Egypt, we shall no more return to this land, but seek another country, to be given to us, over which my people shall be the rulers. The time is set for our departure, and in that hour we must depart, whether Meneptah, our enemy, or Martiesen, our friend, sits on the throne of Egypt."

"And you believe this, Elisheba?"

"Fully, my lord."

"Is it generally believed among your people?"

"There has recently come to life a faith that has long been sleeping, a faith that the God of the Hebrews will take His people out of bondage, and little doubt now exists that the prophets are sent to lead us forth."

Martiesen was lost in thought for several moments, and made no reply, until Elisheba requested permission to depart.

"I have little knowledge of this religion of yours," he said, not heeding her request, "as it has but recently been revived among your people. Tell me, is it true that you have but one God?"

"There is but One."

"And are you to obey this God before all kings or princes?"

Elisheba bowed her head. "It must be so," she said. "But the law is not given us yet. It will be made known when we escape from bondage, for the people of the Hebrew God must be free to serve Him as He shall direct."

"What mighty power would come to Egypt," mused the adon, "if she could enlist the aid of this strange Being, and from the midst of our country banish the senseless objects we have so long regarded as sacred, and with them the lying, deceptive priests! Elisheba, tell me all you know of this God, and where His temple may be found."

"My lord, there is little I can tell. For generations my people have been subject to Egyptians, and have not worshipped at their own altars. Only through tradition has knowledge of the covenant made with Abraham been kept alive, and not until the prophets came to awaken us did we realize that we had a Champion more powerful than all others. Even now little is known of this God, save by the elders chosen out to lead their fellows, of whom, as you know, my father is one. He, my lord, could instruct you."

"Then will I have Darda here, that he may teach not only me, but the princes who will be present at the festivities of this evening. Return to him, Elisheba, and make it known that later in the day

I shall dispatch to Zoan a barge bearing an invitation to Darda and his daughters to become my guests at the fete. The enterprise upon which these princes of the blood have entered is so closely linked with the operations of the Hebrew God that they must be given an opportunity of learning all that may be known concerning Him."

"My lord, it may be that my father may not think it seemly that his daughters attend the banquet of which you speak."

"Have no fear, Elisheba, I have given Darda my word that I would not take you from his home except as wife, and he knows that the Pharaoh has refused my request that you be made free by proclamation. I have hopes that the princes, once they behold your beauty and graciousness, and hear my public declaration, may unite with me in the request, and that thus I may accomplish my heart's fondest desire."

He paused and looked into her eyes.

"What strange spell is this that you have cast over me, Elisheba?" he said tenderly. "I, the adon, Martiesen, who might choose from the noblest women of Egypt, aye, from the royal house itself, am held in thought and action in bondage of love to a simple, modest maiden of the people over whom I am set to rule as a master whose slightest word must be obeyed. This maiden I regard as the noblest of them all. In no other do I see such beauty. My heart beats faster when she is in my sight. Yesterday the noble Zirena came hither with her retinue of twenty barges, surrounded by all the magnificence the daughter of the most powerful prince of our realm may command. Her errand, ostensibly, was to borrow the sacred scarab that has held the post of honor in our family for many generations, which, she hoped, would work a charm to cure her younger sister from a disorder that has long resisted every other agency. Zirena was clad in jewels and garments rich enough to be the ransom of an enslaved nation. The odor of the rarest perfumes of the world filled this conservatory as she moved among my poor blossoms. Amulets of beaten gold, set with precious stones sparkling like the stars of night, and like them without number, clasped her arms and limbs, and a loose network of pearls hung from her shoulders to her waist. She wooed me here, where we are now standing, as was her right. Nay, almost she commanded me to wed her, according to the expressed desire of the Pharaoh, and by every wile of a beautiful woman stirred by passion she enforced her plea. It was a vision almost blinding in its brilliancy, and I was like the bird that hears the soft music of the serpent's low, continuous hiss, and sees the wonderful play of lights upon the arched body and whirling head, which each instant draws nearer and nearer.

"At that moment there came between us the vision of your face, and in an instant the charm was broken. The heavy odors were no longer sweet to my nostrils; the flash of precious stones and the love-glances of melting eyes palled upon my senses, and I knew that neither riches, nor beauty, nor magnificence, nor promise of power could blind my love for you, Elisheba, O fairest pearl in all the realm of Egypt."

Martiesen drew a deep breath and smiled fondly at her. Then, together, they wandered among the lotus plants.

IIIII

CHAPTER V

THE BANQUET

THE princes who came to Martiesen were received as befitted their rank. They had left
Rameses a few hours after the departure of Panas
from that city, having caused a rumor to be
circulated that they were on a pilgrimage to one
of the numerous oracles along the Nile. The
barge upon which the party was conveyed to the
villa was bedecked with splendor seldom
witnessed in modern times. The pavilion was
covered with beaten gold. High above it towered
the fringed sails, checkered in various brilliant
colors. On one was emblazoned the figure of a
vulture, and on the other the fabled phoenix was
wrought in flexible plates of polished bronze. The
fire from which this figure appeared to rise was
formed of golden threads, which, catching the

rays of the sun, sparkled and glistened like living flames. Upon the prow of the barge was carved the head of a lion, and below it, inlaid with patient skill and extreme cunning, gleamed the eye of Osiris. Spicery, balm, and myrrh hung all about the pavilion in small sachets made of colored stuffs, and the air was heavy with their perfume. Huge fans were noiselessly agitated by slave boys, to cool the air. Seated or reclining upon mats or cushions were more than a score of beautiful women, who played upon harps, lyres, guitars, tambourines, or small cymbals, while others, equally beautiful, danced for the amusement of their masters.

Below the main deck was a double gallery, in which were seated the rowers, who aided the almost imperceptible breeze in propelling the craft. They were mostly slaves that had been captured in battle. Their stroke was timed by the master rower, seated amidship, and beating upon a small drum. Their labor, however, was not arduous, for the pilgrimage was leisurely in its character. Stops were made at each town, and the music summoned the inhabitants to assemble upon the river bank and join in the festivities. The scenes on these occasions were crowded with life and color. When the barge had been moored to the stone dock, an orator would step forward, and extol the goodness of the gods and the greatness of Egypt. At intervals, young choristers appeared, and chanted odes calculated to inspire patriotism, and at their conclusion the cymbals would clash, the fanfare of trumpets arise, and then the dancers would spring to their feet, and to the symphony of harp and lute and plaintive pipe tread in graceful measure the figures pleasing alike to gods and men.

Sometimes, from a village before which the barge stopped, a party of its young people came romping to the shore, to take the places of the dancers upon the boat, and the princes bestowed gifts upon the visitors for their entertainment; and at times the steward was directed to arrange for the services of the most beautiful and graceful, who at once took their places upon the deck of the splendid vessel, and accompanied the pleasure party to Martiesen's palace.

In this way, as they approached the adon's villa, Serah was added to the party. Her finely-molded form and beautiful face attracted the attention of Phibis, one of the princes, and when she had danced, a murmur of admiration came from the spectators. Phibis directed that Serah be brought before him, and he inquired whether she was willing to accompany the party. He was told that she would not go unless her mother, a famous soothsayer, were permitted to join the company. The woman was Masarah, a Hebrew, the widow of an Egyptian physician, and one of her powers of divination was supposed to lie in her ability to read, from the flowers of the lotus, the coming of events, either good or evil. When she came upon the barges, Masarah approached the reclining nobles, and to each gave a lotus flower, freshly plucked from the stalk. Bidding them look into the flowers intently, the woman waited a moment; and then took the blossoms in her hand. She examined them with care.

"My lords," she said, "Masarah would not from choice be the bearer of evil portents in a time of festivity and happiness, but she speaks what she reads. In all these flowers, I see only darkness. I cannot discover what it hides, for the veil will not open to my eyes."

"Darkness is welcome," laughed Phibis. "It follows every day, and brings both pleasure and rest."

"Yes, my lord," replied the woman, "but not

every day is followed by a darkness like that which is to come."

"Nor is every day as bright and full of music as the one that is here," declared Phibis. "Let the night be what it may, the day is with us, and we will enjoy it to the glory of the gods. Serah pleases us to a greater degree than her mother."

He gave a signal, and the dancing girl leaped to the center of the pavilion, a gleaming figure of delightful airiness and graceful poses. The sails were spread to the soft winds, the music rose upon the perfume-laden atmosphere, the steady beating of the oars broke the waters of the Nile into sparkling waves, and the varicolored barge, forming a vision of unwonted beauty, moved upon its course.

Thus journeying, they came to the house of Martiesen. The mild, balmy night had commenced to deepen from twilight, when the barge, all aglow with mellow lights, and pulsating with music and the preparations for disembarking, approached the landing-place. The blare of cymbals and trumpets on the shore gave the signal to numbers of men and boys, who ran along both sides of a grand approach, and with their torches put fire to the wicks of innumerable swinging lamps of bronze. The approach was lined by a double row of small obelisks and sphinxes, mysterious compounds of the human form and that of the lion and the ram, denoting the union of strength and intellect in gods and men. Two colossal figures in the attitude of profound repose stood beside the entrance, which was a lofty pylon, or porch. Through this gateway admission was gained to a spacious court, open to the sky and surrounded by colonnades. As the princes and their retinue of musicians, dancers, attendants, and slaves filed into this court, their music ceased, and when the last note died away, a magnificent curtain, upon which was wrought in embroidery an infinite number of hieroglyphic characters, rolled back from an open vestibule leading to the audience or banqueting room.

A wave of music poured forth; choristers lifted their voices in happy unison; slaves swung heavy lamps in front of polished tablets of silver, gold, and marble; children garlanded with flowers ran through the colonnades waving sachets of costly perfumes, while, from apartments at the right and left, girls issued forth and bestowed luxurious wreaths upon their visitors. Then the princes moved through the vestibule, and entered the banquet-chamber. The great room was crowded with splendor. Small obelisks were ranged on both sides, and their perfectly polished and exquisitely colored surfaces reflected the light thrown upon them through sheets of emerald and amber or eyelets of white coral. To heighten this effect, a mellow radiance glowed from openings near the carved and enameled ceiling. Six great battle-paintings were ranged in series upon the walls back of the obelisks. The glitter of the beaten gold-leaf upon their war chariots, the brilliance of coloring, which gave the animation of life to every figure represented, together with the heroic size of the men, animals, and weapons, all active in the terrific struggle of a fearful encounter, formed a background that quickened the pulses of the warlike men whose eyes turned toward the representations.

Tablets filled the spaces between the paintings, and inscriptions told in simple language the stories of wars prosecuted and victories won by the valor of Martiesen and his ancestors.

In the center of the hall, upon a dais, or platform, of marble, the adon sat in almost regal state. Two giant Ethiopians, clad in burnished trappings, stood at the back of his chair, while at his feet, in sharp contrast with the giant blacks, crouched two Numidian dwarfs. Around the platform, seated on tabourets, were rows of women with harps and lutes. On the steps leading to the dais was a guard under the command of Panas, the lieutenant. The robes of state worn by the adon were of the finest linen, embroidered with the insignia of his rank. About his neck was a heavy chain of gold, his badge of office and the gift of the king. To this was attached the eye of Osiris, wrought of precious stones fastened together in the most skillful manner. Bands of gold and silver were clasped upon his arms and ankles, and at his side, attached to a girdle ornamented with gems, hung the dagger of the Libyan.

As the princes approached the dais, the adon rose and received each with a kindly greeting. Then, bestowing upon each a golden ring bearing figures of Ammon and Ptah, a sphinx, a lion, or sacred serpent, he placed them in the hands of the attendants. A signal was given, and while music filled the hall, the visitors were conducted to their apartments, to make preparations for the feast.

At an Egyptian banquet there was none of that riotous debauchery so common among the Greeks and Romans at later periods. The guests were anointed by their slaves, and over their shoulders or upon their heads were placed garlands of flowers. They sat on low seats, or reclined on cushions and mats, with circular pieces of polished wood hollowed out for head-rests. The courses, though abundant and numerous, were most simple, and were served with deliberation and in decent order. The wine was light and not intoxicating. It was contained in porous jars, which were swung and fanned at the same time by slaves in the galleries, that the liquor might be cool and sparkling. While the food was served, groups of women and girls performed upon elaborately wrought harps and lutes, or men played upon the single, double, or oblong flute. There were many songs, or, more strictly speaking, odes, written by poets or priests for the occasion; the themes were nearly always those extolling the gods, or the valor of the host or of his guests. Gymnastic exhibitions were introduced between the courses, or the antics of dwarfs amused the assembled guests. There was always dancing, performed by scores of girls, who

sometimes danced in concert, but more frequently in couples or alone. And among all the
dancers before the adon and his guests, there was
none who more completely filled the eye, or to
whom was given greater acclaim, than Serah, the
daughter of Masarah.

||||||

CHAPTER VI

APPREHENSION

SOME hours before the arrival of his guests, the adon summoned his secretary, and dictated a letter of invitation to Darda, requesting the Hebrew to be present with his daughters at the banquet. He then directed the dispatch of messengers on a light barge to Zoan in time to return with the party before the banquet should commence. Other missions were also entrusted to the scribe, and then the adon turned his attention to the preparations going forward on all sides. Engrossed in the numerous demands upon his time in the afternoon and early evening, Martiesen did not notice the absence of Peshala, or the failure of the Hebrew and his daughters to appear. But when the guests were seated, and the host made the round of his guests, to see that all were properly provided, the vacant places were observed. Summoning Panas to his side, Martiesen requested that inquiry be made of the scribe as to what messengers had been sent to Zoan, and why they had not returned.

The adon moved constantly among his guests, watching zealously that their comfort might not be neglected. He conversed with certain of the princes upon the matters divulged to him by Panas earlier in the day. Phibis made known to him further details, and together they discussed the chances of success or failure. The adon did not possess the enthusiasm they expected to find in him, but he admitted the gravity of the situation and the necessity for action of some character. He desired a few hours for further consideration, and promised that before his guests departed, he would give them his answer. He hoped to consult with Darda, should the occasion offer, and for this reason he put off his decision.

But why was the Hebrew not present; or, if he could not come, why was there no message? As these questions arose, and the absence of Panas was lengthened beyond what appeared to be a reasonable time, Martiesen grew apprehensive.

When the lieutenant was finally observed near the entrance, the adon abruptly excused himself to Phibis, and hastened to the doorway. Panas reported that the barge had been dispatched in charge of an Assyrian slave named Bariet, accompanied by an Ethiopian dwarf. Peshala was not in the villa. No one recalled having seen him after he handed Bariet a roll of papyrus at the landing, with instructions to deliver the message to Darda of Zoan. It was thought that he returned to his apartments, but when these were examined, evidences of his recent presence were wanting. Two slaves and a light boat were also missing, but this was not unusual, for in so large an establishment there were servants who would take advantage of the confusion attendant upon a festival of this nature to escape work by stealing away, trusting their absence would not be noticed by their busily-occupied overseers.

Though wondering at the disappearance of the Libyan, Panas had no thought of danger to those expected from Zoan. To the adon, however, came a fear that he could not shake off. He ordered two trustworthy guardsmen to take a boat and row at least halfway to Zoan, and allow no boat to pass without ascertaining the identity of its occupants. He also directed that the search for

Peshala be thorough, and a patrol be started upon the river bank in both directions.

On returning to his guests, Martiesen found it impossible to bring his mind to the things immediately before him. He was preoccupied and distraught. He heard the music, but through its notes came the low, deep voice of Elisheba, imploring him for help. He saw the dancers, but to Martiesen their waving arms were lifted in appeal, and their supple limbs were bent in prayer. He ate, but could not name the taste or substance of that of which he partook. Jest and song, and praise in poem or prose were poured into his ears, and though Martiesen smiled and bowed, or murmured his thanks, he could not tell the next moment what he had heard. Only when Panas came did Martiesen show interest, but Panas brought no tidings that gave the adon rest. Finally the lieutenant told him that the searching boat had returned without result, and he asked if the guardsmen should be given instructions to proceed to Zoan.

"No, Panas. The night draws to a close, and the end of the feast will soon be announced. Then I shall be free to unravel this mystery. Until that time, though the Nile turn in its channel and run back to its source, I may not leave my guests.

Stand ready to accompany me."

It was customary for the master of the festivities connected with an Egyptian feast to watch for the coming of the dawn, and at the time of its first appearance, he would enter the banquet-hall and announce the conclusion of the banquet. Immediately thereafter all vessels containing food were put aside, and wine was poured for each guest. Then slaves entered, with the figure of an elaborately painted and gilded mummy stretched upon a sledge. As it was slowly drawn before the silent guests, the master of the ceremony addressed the company thus:

"Looking upon this, drink and enjoy thyself; for such shalt thou be when thou art dead."

The master of Martiesen's feast waited long. Often his eyes sought the eastern horizon, but no ray of light rewarded his vigil. With startled senses he endeavored in vain to discover the position of the fixed stars; but only gloom and impenetrable darkness met his gaze.

The music palled upon the guests. The feats of the acrobats failed to hold their attention. Food or wine served by slaves shambling with weariness remained untasted, or fell upon the floor. The dancers were slow and awkward after their exertions of the night, and no longer caught the

eye or won acclaim. Drooping and wilted garlands were strewn upon the couches, or hung in
shapeless strings about the necks of the wearers.
The nearly exhausted oil in many lamps gave out
a sickening odor. Anxiety and fear touched every
heart, for all knew the hour was past when the
feast should close. But no light yet appeared.

The adon summoned the master of the festival
to his side, and inquired if he could not discern
the approach of day.

"My lord, all is gloom and heavy darkness.
Though the hour of its birth has expired, the day
is not approaching."

The adon was now seated upon the dais, and
the princes and those who had furnished the
night's entertainment crowded to his side.
Wonder looked out of their eyes, and terror
blanched their cheeks. Over the multitude rested
a hush like that of death.

"My guests," said the adon, with a calmness that
inspired some degree of courage in them, "I do
not know the explanation of the mystery that has
come upon us. The master of the feast declares
that without there is no appearance of the dawn,
though well you know that the hour of its
breaking is past. I ask that all save the princes
retire to their apartments, and there await the

unraveling of this phenomenon."

"Nay, my lord adon, it is a trick of the gods to prolong our pleasure," cried one who had drunk too often and deep of the wine. "Send the cup around again, and let the dancers take their places."

"Silence, man!" replied one at his side, with trembling voice. "Have you no fear in such a time as this?"

"Let an oracle be brought," said another. "Where is the woman who came upon the barge with the queen of the dancers?"

"Aye, where is the soothsayer, she who read the message in the lotus flowers?" called several other voices.

"Did she not predict a night such as we had never seen when we were coming hither through the sunshine? Now make her tell when the day will come," said another.

"Masarah! Masarah!" shouted Phibis. "That is the name of the hag, and she was present not long since. Demand of her what charm she has cast, my lord, for she had an evil way."

Those who stood near Masarah pushed back from her side, and she was alone in front of the adon.

"Woman," he demanded, "have you an

explanation of this mystery?"

"My lord adon, I have a message."

"Then, in the name of the gods, stand forth and declare it."

"Not in the name of the gods," said Masarah, coming forward and stepping upon the dais, "but in the name of the God of the Hebrews! He has sent upon all this land of Egypt a darkness which may be felt. Only in the dwellings of His people shall there be light."

Then fell upon that scene of revelry a gloom that dimmed lamp, and gem, and polished marble, or glittering gold and silver. Strong men tottered and laid hold upon each other for support; women, dumb and trembling, sank to the floor, and groveled aimlessly in their bedraggled finery; slaves crept to the feet of their masters and moaned in piteous terror. Confusion took the place of order, and hearts that never before had quailed were now weak with fear!

Tangible danger in its most threatening form is not so terrifying as the thing that steals upon us, we know not whence, in a shape that may not be weighed, or measured, or defined. The one may be resisted, even though we know the odds are overwhelming, and resistance is hopeless. In the very act of striving is found some outlet for the despair that bears against us. With the unseen danger we cannot cope, and, horror-stricken, we feel its awful presence without knowing which way to turn for aid.

Thus it was with those present at this feast, and to more than one came the fear that death stood near, or had thrown his black veil over them with a sure and irresistible hand.

One man spoke, and his voice, though strident and commanding, trembled with terror.

"Strike down the hag! Strike down the hag!" he shouted; and yet made no move to execute his own commands, though Masarah was almost at his side.

"Let no one do violence," said Martiesen, quickly, "for it is not the work of the woman. A Mightier One than the soothsayers, or the priests, or than all the gods of Egypt, has visited us with His anger. Masarah is not to blame. Indeed, it is to her that we must look for guidance. Woman, where lies our escape?"

"It is not given me to know, my lord," replied Masarah. "Only this I know, that those who resist the Hebrew God must feel His anger."

"Have you no counsel?"

"My lord, I would counsel patience. Let the

princes be conducted to their rooms, where they may rest in quietness. Serah and I will lead the women to their apartments, and calm them as best we may. But all must await the working of the will that has turned the day of Egypt into blackest night."

Assisted by Panas and others who still retained some measure of calm, the adon succeeded in conducting his noble guests to the chambers prepared for their reception. Their slaves and attendants clung in mute fear to those from whom they had some right to expect protection, nor could they be shaken off until they were permitted to be near their masters, and cling to the silken hangings of their couches as to a life-line that would guide them to safety.

Masarah and Serah did not falter; with brave words they encouraged the women to accompany them to the portion of the villa that had been set apart for their refreshment. They worked rapidly, until the great banquet-hall was cleared, and its splendor was silent in the fearful gloom.

||||||

CHAPTER VII

DARKNESS

To Martiesen there came no thought of rest. Even while he was engaged in reassuring his guests, he resolved to proceed to Zoan as soon as he might be free to do so. The appearance of this weird, unnatural darkness furnished him with a further reason for immediate action. He would first assure himself of the safety of Elisheba; then he would seek the Hebrew prophets, and from them learn what they might tell concerning this distressing visitation. And then, if possible, he would retrace his journey, and proceed to Rameses, and make personal appeal to the Pharaoh. Under present conditions the king might give ear to his advice.

It was decided that Panas should remain in charge of the household, and the adon, accom-

panied by the giant Ethiopians, who often served
as his bodyguard, would essay the trip to Zoan.
But when they departed from the portico, a
difficulty arose. From the numerous lamps and
tapers there was some light within the building,
but the darkness outside was so intense that they
could not determine the direction they were
taking, and found themselves wandering among
the columns lining the approach. The flickering
blaze of their torch burned dull and red in the
thick and lifeless atmosphere, casting a circle of
dim light only a pace or two in diameter. From
all objects and substances the power of radiation
had been withdrawn; the air itself, laden with an
impalpable mist, stifled and deadened the rays of
light at their very source.

Guided by the voice of Panas, who was peering
in wonder upon the darkness from the portico,
the adon and his Ethiopians retraced their steps.

"My lord," said the lieutenant, "it is madness
for you to attempt this journey. You would
immediately lose direction upon the river, and
once adrift you will not know where to land."

"And it will be madness to remain here with
haunting fears constantly arising in my mind.
Nor will I remain, even though I crawl upon the

river bank. Where is the woman?"

"The soothsayer, my lord?"

"Aye, Masarah; seek her, I pray you, at once, and bid her come to the portico."

"She is near at hand," replied Panas. Groping a few paces within the entrance, the lieutenant called to Masarah, and soon returned, accompanied by her and her daughter.

"Masarah, are you not of the Hebrews?" asked the adon.

"I am, my lord, a sister of Darda."

"Then would it not be possible for you to guide me to Zoan?"

"My lord," she replied after a moment's hesitation, "the same Power that has sent this darkness upon your land, has withheld it from the homes of the Hebrews, and has given to those of that blood some freedom from the punishment. If your mission be one upon which my people would look with favor, I shall endeavor to guide you upon the way. I doubt not that I may do it with safety."

Martiesen briefly explained the urgent necessity, and when Masarah learned that there was reason to fear for the safety of her brother and his children, she was eager to depart. Taking a long silken sash from her waist, she placed one end of the fabric in the adon's hands. She then ranged Panas and Serah upon either side, and put the remaining end of the sash into the hands of the Ethiopians. Returning to the adon, Masarah took him by the arm, and without hesitancy led the way directly to the landing. Here the woman bade her charges remain motionless, and they heard her moving among the boats. Soon she called to Serah, and directed her to conduct the adon to the boat. With a word of farewell to Panas, the adon, guided by the gentle touch of the girl, moved cautiously down the steps. Reaching out his hands to Masarah, he was aided to a seat in a light phaselus, constructed of papyrus, and made watertight with bitumen. In like manner the Ethiopians were seated, and paddles were thrust into their hands. A few words passed between the mother and daughter; a command was given to the slaves to dip their paddles; the boat rocked with a steady movement, and the adon, reaching over the prow into the water, felt a glad thrill, as he realized that they were moving out upon the surface of the Nile.

"Is Serah in the phaselus?" asked Martiesen.

"She is not," replied Masarah, who sat at the

stern, using a light oar for a rudder.

"My daughter remains to guide your lieutenant on his return to the villa and to give such assistance as she may in caring for those who were your guests, but are now prisoners at your home. She will be needed to quiet and comfort the women, who were so greatly stricken with fear."

"And surely Panas will be fully occupied in caring for the princes and servants," replied the adon, whose courage rose with each moment of progress. "They were filled with desire for flight, and yet they knew not which way to run. Awe struck every heart, and indeed it is no wonder, for the dread cloud came upon us like the end of all things. Never on the battlefield have I seen men so wrought upon with terror, nor did there ever come to my own heart a greater weakness. Until you brought me to myself, by pointing out the piteous plight in which my guests were thrown, I was incapable of motion or speech."

The woman made no answer, except to order the blacks to increase their stroke, and to assure them that they need have no fears.

"And Panas also was frightened," continued the adon, as though extracting a crumb of comfort from that circumstance. "Never before have I seen him tremble! But when the lights grew dim, and that wail of mortal fear arose from those about us, Panas grasped my arm, as if to say that we had often faced danger side by side, and would not shrink from it now. I recall that his hand shook as with palsy; nor did it stop until Serah came to him, and with a word sent him to the guests. How they worked to calm the tumult, Serah and Panas, not neglecting the meanest slave! I saw them in that dim light everywhere, and let me tell you, Masarah, as they strove together, they came to know each other, and I fear that the brave Panas, even in that time of terror, did not lose sight of his love for the dancing-girl. It need be no surprise to you if they come together upon your return, and beg consent to marry."

Still there was no answer from Masarah, and without encouragement to speak, the adon relapsed into silence.

It was now past the midday. Martiesen believed that they were keeping near the river bank, but of this he had no positive knowledge, save that which came through sounds borne upon the heavy air. The lowing cattle, tethered in pens which the owners could not approach in the blighting blackness of this terrible plague, called for the light which they knew was overlong in coming. Neighing chariot horses, in the villages where a few military forces were quartered, sent out cries more distressing than those heard from wounded beasts upon the field of battle. Dogs howled in doleful measure, and grunting swine, running hither and thither with the fear that possessed all creatures, often plunged into the river or some of the canals, and sank beneath the waters. Nor were evidences wanting of the fear that laid hold upon man, for appealing cries arose from many a lonely hut, or swelled in volume from assemblages where people in some manner had found their way to a common center.

At intervals it was observed that attempts were made to dispel the gloom, for dim fires of dry weeds and sedge were discovered upon the river bank. Like the torch at the villa, they burned with a dull, red glow, and their beams extended but a few paces beyond the center. Crowds of frightened beings strove with each other for a place nearest the flames. There was no longer class or distinction. Priests, warriors, judges, architects, chiefs of districts, laborers, peasants, slaves, even the dreaded and hated embalmers, huddled together, a shivering, moaning mass, and the hand of no man was raised against his brother because of caste. There was only strife to draw near to the almost lifeless flames, so great was the thirst for light. Women and children were brushed aside without pity, and their fearful cries were borne out upon the black-laden air.

Sometimes the boat in which the adon sat plowed through flocks of waterfowl hovering together upon the bosom of the river, and when this happened, the fluttering of the birds and their discordant clamor struck such terror to the Ethiopians that the slaves were with difficulty prevented from leaping overboard. Masarah seldom spoke, and then but a word or two of caution or command; the adon, impatient and awestruck as he contemplated the unnatural conditions, was silent and absorbed in his own thoughts. Thus, guided by the strange power given the Hebrew woman and withheld from the others, the craft went forward in safety.

It was three hours by the river in daylight from the home of the adon to Zoan. In this day of more than midnight darkness, when all Egypt was shrouded with a veil which the sun could not pierce, a much longer time was consumed in the journey, and the hour was approaching when night should have fallen, when Masarah quickly turned the boat to the right, and bade the slaves cease rowing. With extreme caution she guided the boat to the bank, which at this point was high and abrupt, and finally came to the landing-place. This was built of granite blocks, with a perpendicular face to the river, and the adon felt carefully along the wall, until the narrow stairway was found, and they disembarked. Again employing the silken scarf to keep the party together, the woman led the way, straight back from the Nile, along a beaten path. After a few minutes, Masarah drew the adon's attention to a faint glimmer in the windows of a house near at hand. She approached the door, and struck upon it nervously. There was no reply, and, after waiting a moment, the woman struck again. "Open! It is Masarah and the adon Martiesen," she called.

With little delay the door was opened, and they entered a room, as brilliant with light as the noontime of any day in the Egyptian summer.

|||||||

CHAPTER VIII

AT MY LORD'S REQUEST

FOR the greater part of an entire day Martiesen had been surrounded by complete darkness, and when he stepped into the flood of light pervading the Hebrew house, he was so blinded by its brilliancy that for several moments he could not distinguish the objects before him.

He had entered a large, square apartment of considerable height, with several small windows near the ceiling for the purpose of ventilation, rather than for any design they might serve in providing light. A stairway in one corner led to the roof, where it was the custom of the family to spend the night. Unlike the houses of the Egyptians, the stucco walls and ceilings were not ornamented with paintings, for the Hebrews were a race in bondage. A few of the simplest cooking utensils hung under the stairway, and bricks were piled near them in crude resemblance to a modern fireplace or oven.

Seated upon low, rude stools near the center of the room were nearly a score of grave, heavy, burden-bent men. They were clad in loose, coarse, sleeveless cotton garments reaching their knees, and wore sandals. Their hair was long, matted, and unkempt. Upon their hands and arms were stains of clay and bruises of stubble, for they were the Hebrew brickmakers, who daily performed their tasks under the eyes of the Pharaoh's relentless masters. Grouped in a circle, upon a few coarse mats at the rear of the room, were the women and children, poorly-clad, half-fed creatures, who went to the brick-yards with the men, or wandered abroad through the fields in search of straw to be used in the manufacture of the bricks. Upon all there fell a hush when Masarah and her charges entered.

The scene was not unfamiliar to the adon, for, in his intercourse with the Hebrews as the governor of their nome, he often visited them in their homes, or met them thus for consultation. He knew that these rough and uncouth-looking people lacked neither character nor intelligence.

For many generations the Hebrews were leaders in the arts, sciences, achievements in agriculture, the military, and commerce, and not until a dynasty arose which feared their power and influence, were they driven from these honorable vocations, and reduced to the most servile bondage. But as the adon gazed upon the Hebrews assembled in the light that filled this house from some mysterious force, he detected in their faces a gleam of hope, which he had never before observed.

The Hebrews arose, and stood before him out of respect for the governor of the nome, and when his eyes could bear the light, the adon saw them there and courteously acknowledged their greeting. Darda, in whose house he stood, approached and bade him welcome.

"Darda," said the adon, trembling with anxiety, "is Elisheba with you?"

"Elisheba, my lord! Is she not at the villa?"

Then the heart of Martiesen stood still, for in this question of the startled father he read it all, and the fears which come crowding upon us when those for whom we have the greatest love are in the midst of peril, rained their heavy blows upon his senses, and made him sick and faint, and killed his hope. He attempted to speak, but no words came. Darda turned to Masarah, and sought an explanation.

"We came to find her here, she was not at the festival," was all the woman could answer.

The old man would have fallen, had not his friends sustained him, and led him to a seat. In the few words spoken he read danger, treachery, perhaps shame.

"They came, my lord, and brought me your respectful message, requesting that I, with my daughters, should attend the festival."

"Who bore this message, Darda? Who bore this message?" demanded the adon.

"Your secretary — the scribe Peshala."

"As I thought — as I feared! Traitorous Peshala, against whom Elisheba warned me, and I could not see his infamy!" And Martiesen clenched his hands, and beat upon his breast.

"I could not go to the villa at that time," continued Darda, "for the prophets had given commands to the elders to assemble in the evening when the tasks were finished, when important messages were to be given. Intending to follow later in the night, I consented to the departure of Elisheba and Abigail, her sister.

And yet, I know not why, I feared their going."

"O that your fears had kept them by your side, or that your God might have reached out His hand to save these innocents from this monstrous plotter!"

Martiesen paced the floor in impotent anger, trembling with the passion that possessed him, and glaring into the faces of the men about him, who were hushed to silence by the evidences of his great distress and consuming wrath. He sought a sign of hope or comfort in their countenances, but found neither. Then his sinewy form stiffened as with sudden resolution, and he stood before them, a towering spirit of vengeance.

"Men of the Hebrews, and you, women, who have voices and tears, cry unto your God and implore Him to palsy the hands and bind the limbs of this monster, to hold this beast fettered, until I may search out his place of hiding, and bring your maidens unsullied from his grasp!"

Before any could interfere, Martiesen turned and dashed through the door into the darkness.

Crazed by the knowledge that Elisheba was in the gravest peril, the adon had but one thought — the pursuit of Peshala. Inactivity would mean death or insanity. The calm and deliberate organization of a search for the abductor would have been an impossibility. Every fiber of his body was stirred to action, and his absorbing love for the woman whom he believed to be in greatest peril rushed in where reason and prudence should have prevailed, and urged him forward and ever forward.

So, when he burst from the lighted room into the night, the adon did not pause or hesitate. Straight ahead he went, without knowing or even considering the direction, but believing that steps, bounds, leaps, on, on, whithersoever they might take him, would lead to the object of his wrath. One hand at his side grasped the handle of the Libyan dagger, which he had worn as an ornament at his festival; the other was extended with fingers half-clenched, as if to seize and hold the false scribe, until he should sink dead at the feet of the avenger. Every nerve was vibrating and tense, but all senses, save that which cried for vengeance, were dulled.

Voices from the crowded doorway called upon him through the darkness to return; but Martiesen gave them no heed. Stumbling often, yet regardless of all, he pressed forward upon his course. He slipped and fell headlong down the oozy side of an irrigating ditch, but rose from the soft mud in the bottom to mount the opposite bank with a bound. Thick running vines caught about his ankles, and pulled him to his knees, but he cut the obstructions away with the sharp blade, and sprang forward again to recover the time that had been lost by his fall.

Thus the adon came to the Nile and saw it not, nor heard the ripple of its sluggish waters. He was running steadily now, for the earth along the river bank was trodden smooth and firm. Without warning or thought of danger, he leaped free from the precipitous bank, and sank beneath the water. In a moment he came to the surface, and struck blindly forward, to swim as he had run. The hand with which he clasped the dagger hilt drew the weapon from its sheath, and did not loose its hold. As he was borne along with steady sweeps, the sharp blade struck and cut a great gash in the papyrus shell in which he came to Zoan. By this time he was growing calmer. The sudden plunge into the river in a measure restored him to a realization of the perils with which he was beset. He knew that there was a desperate struggle for life before him, and so he laid hold upon the frail craft, and attempted to draw himself over its prow. In this he had nearly succeeded, and was putting forth a final effort, when the water rushed into the boat through the hole made by the weapon, and the adon was whirled once more underneath the water.

Again he fought his way to the surface, but now his breath was coming in painful gasps, and his stroke was quick and nerveless. Frenzy gave way to despair, and the thought came to Martiesen that he would sink there in the depths of Father Nile, and might never again look upon his beloved country. New strength was born with this thought. It was a spur to greater effort — he must not die there like a malefactor, when so much depended upon his living. If there were only a point of light or a sound to guide him, he might reach the shore; but in this darkness, and with no sound, save that caused by his strokes and his panting breath, he was bewildered and swam in a circle.

At length his hands struck against the stones which formed the landing-place, and with the touch hope returned. He felt along the slimy face of the granite wall, seeking a crevice into which he might thrust his fingers, and raise himself to the edge of the dock; but the workmen had performed their task too well. He tossed above him the dagger to which he had so closely clung until this moment, and heard its ringing fall upon the steps. Now he would climb to it, and with it at his side once more, he would move with caution, until he might secure a boat with which to follow this accursed Libyan. With supreme effort he leaped clear of the water, and secured a slender hold upon the sharp edge of the wall. Inch by inch the struggling man drew himself slowly from the water. The muscles upon his shoulders and arms stood out in knotted bunches; in his ears, like the rushing wind, roared the hot, pulsating stream of life.

At the very edge he poised, but the utmost limit of exertion had been reached. From his lips came one agonized cry of despair — and Martiesen fell backward into the Nile.

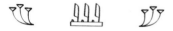

||||||||

CHAPTER IX

WHEN Peshala received the commission to invite Darda and his daughters to the festival, he at once formed a plan for the abduction of Elisheba. He anticipated that in carrying out his designs he might be compelled to murder the aged Hebrew, but this did not deter him from his purpose. Peshala had by no means been idle during his months of service as the adon's secretary. He had made preparations to take advantage of just such an occasion as this by building up a certain following among the servants. One whom he had selected was Bariet, an Assyrian who had been captured in battle some years before, and was purchased by Martiesen as a slave. Although Bariet's left hand had been struck off — the customary treatment of prisoners who might be retained as slaves — he used his maimed arm with dexterity, and possessed great strength. Another whom the secretary had enlisted in his cause was an Ethiopian dwarf, a creature who could best be controlled through fear, and whose strength and agility were marvelous. These two were directed to make the preparations which the secretary thought necessary for carrying out his evil intentions. A quantity of food was placed in a small boat, which two slaves were ordered to row to a point some distance up the river on the western bank, there to await the arrival of Bariet. Then, after agreeing upon a place in the direction of Zoan where he might be found, Peshala secretly left the villa, and hurried down the river. At the appointed time, Bariet and the dwarf departed with the barge upon their well-understood errand. At the place agreed upon, Peshala was taken aboard, and they reached Zoan late in the afternoon, the apparently accredited and trusted messengers of Martiesen.

Like all Hebrew women, Elisheba and her younger sister Abigail were often employed at work in the gardens, and they were thus engaged when the secretary approached and delivered the message of his master. It was not unexpected, but the girl was disturbed because the adon had placed the execution of his commission in the hands of Peshala. True, she had never until that morning found reasons upon which to base her suspicions of the Libyan, though she had long feared and distrusted him. He had ever been respectful, grave, dignified, and apparently obedient to his master. She had heard him express pity and regret over the unhappy lot of the Hebrews; but that subtle faculty which we explain as intuition, and which may be the warnings whispered by those whose eyes have been opened to all things, and who see our danger, told her that he was a man to fear. At no time in her life had this voice of warning sounded more distinctly to Elisheba than at this moment.

Darda was summoned from the place where thousands toiled, and the papyrus roll was placed in his hands. It was customary upon festival occasions for nobles or officials to open their houses to very large companies, and in his younger days Darda had been present at numerous banquets given by Martiesen's father. It was his wish to attend this one, as he possessed a pardonable pride in the distinction shown him by

the adon's invitation, and he had also a desire
that his daughters might look upon a scene of so
much beauty. However, during the afternoon,
word had been passed from mouth to mouth that
messengers from the prophets were at hand, and
Darda had been told that the elders would
assemble in the evening to receive the commands. Promising to follow at a later hour, Darda
bade his daughters robe themselves in their finest
linen and return with Peshala. The simple preparations were quickly made, and as the sun
dipped below the barren peaks which shut off the
mysterious western desert, Elisheba and Abigail
took places in the gaily-caparisoned craft, and
Peshala gave his slaves the command to row.

The Libyan sat in the stern of the boat and
directed its course. At first they moved at
customary speed, for Bariet and the dwarf were
sturdy oarsmen, but they had proceeded scarcely
an hour from Zoan before the speed was
slackened, and in the gathering darkness they
passed midstream and drew nearer the westerly
bank of the river. Elisheba, distrustful and
apprehensive from the start, noted this circumstance, though she did not make known her fears
to Abigail. She watched closely every movement,

and bravely kept up her playful manner with her sister.

The night was now fallen. Lights appeared on the river bank, and sent their shafts dancing across the water. Far ahead, on the eastern bank; was discerned a considerable illumination, which Elisheba knew to be the house of the adon Martiesen; and yet the silent figure in the stern of the barge did not point the craft in that direction, but hugged the shadows of the western shore. Elisheba arose, and approached him.

"Why is the barge not turned toward your master's landing?" she inquired.

"We are not expected so early, my lady. Indeed, should we not appear at all, the feast will not be delayed; nor will it be less merry to all save one."

In this answer, all his black villainy was revealed to the girl. Her limbs trembled with sudden weakness, fear filled her heart, and she grasped her sister's shoulder for support.

"What is it, sister?" asked Abigail, half rising to Elisheba's side. "What does Peshala say?"

"Hush, Abigail, and remain here near me, for we are in peril," whispered Elisheba. "For some purpose of his own the secretary has decoyed us on this journey, and is now taking us beyond the villa."

Turning to the slaves she said: "My sister and I were bidden to the festival prepared by your master, and he expects you to bring us safe to his villa. In his name I command you to row the barge to his landing-place with all speed. If you fail in this, and give aid to whatever evil designs Peshala may have, the anger and punishment of your master will be upon you. If you obey what I have commanded, I myself will see that your reward is a noble one."

A cold, sneering laugh from the Libyan was the reply. "These men, my lady, are no longer slaves, as are the Hebrew maidens. With me they have thrown off the yoke of Martiesen, the traitor to his king, and have no regard for his commands, either delivered by himself or by the lips which he so dearly covets. Ere the sun shall rise and set upon Egypt, we will make his plottings known to the ruler he hopes to supplant, and in the division of his property, neither the men with me nor myself will be forgotten."

Elisheba could not reply, for her heart nearly ceased its beating, and her tongue refused to frame the words. The secretary arose, and came near her side.

"Sit down," he said, not ungently, "and accept your lot; for be assured, great honor awaits you. You shall be returned to the palace that is now Martiesen's, and shall be received there with all the splendor due to one of your beauty and the rank you are to occupy. I have the proofs that Martiesen is engaged in a plot to usurp the throne, and in person I will convey them to the Pharaoh. It was no idle boast which I made this morning, and if you will it, the fact that you spurned me shall be forgotten and forgiven. If not, then you are still my slave. Upon whom do you think the king will bestow his gratitude when this plot is uncovered, if not upon Peshala? And who is there with whom Peshala will more willingly share his honors than with Elisheba, the most beautiful of all the maidens of Zoan? Though scorned and driven from her presence by threats, the Libyan can forget the slight in his hour of triumph, if the Hebrew woman will press upon his lips one sweet caress of love."

He was bending close over her, his face lighted with that devilish passion and cunning which he so largely possessed. With all the strength of her supple, well-trained muscles, to which were added the fear and abhorrence with which she regarded her captor, Elisheba sprang full upon him, and sank her fingers into his face. The unexpected assault carried Peshala backwards over the side of the boat. Holding to him with the ferocity and desperation of one who fights for more than life, Elisheba plunged headlong with her enemy into the river.

A scream from Abigail rang over the water as she attempted to follow her sister, but the dwarf caught her around the waist, and with his broad hand upon her mouth, choked her back under the canopy of the barge. Bariet was peering into the water, and as the struggling man and woman came to the surface, the slave swung himself over the side, and swam rapidly toward them. He dealt the girl a blow upon the head that stunned her, and when Peshala shook himself from her grasp, they together dragged her insensible form into the boat. The arms and ankles of the sisters were then bound, and strips of sail-cloth were tied over their mouths. Then the dwarf gave attention to bathing and bandaging the jagged, bleeding wound in the Libyan's face. His left eye was nearly torn from its socket, and extending down his sallow cheeks were cuts as deep as though made by the claws of a tiger.

But there was little time for delay. The scream uttered by Abigail might have been heard by the boats ever plying upon the river. Indeed, several of these were near at hand, and were filled with revelers on their way to the festival. Only the music, songs, and laughter of their occupants prevented Abigail's call for help from attracting attention. Silently the men resumed their oars; the barge went on its way, leaving the dancing lights and tinkling music far in its wake — forward into the darkness, with no word spoken by the desperate captors. A low, smothered moan of agony came from Elisheba as she recovered consciousness, and realized that her fight for death and, through its door, liberty, was lost. Peshala went forward and bent his bandaged face down, until his hot breath scorched her cheeks. "Mine! Mine!" he hissed. "Before the very eyes of your lover Martiesen I will parade you — a captive mistress, my suppliant, broken slave!"

An hour passed, and upon a signal from Peshala the slaves ceased their rapid strokes, and the boat drew slowly nearer the western bank. They proceeded thus but a few moments, when Bariet in a low tone drew the secretary's attention

to another boat a short distance ahead. Peshala
cautiously guided the barge to its side, and made
sure that the occupants were the slaves whom
Bariet had dispatched thither with supplies.
Reaching over the prow of the barge, Bariet held
the smaller boat as if awaiting an order from his
master. Peshala stepped lightly down between the
slaves, and without a word of warning his arm
rose above his head, a polished blade flashed in
the pale light of the stars, and the bending figure
nearest him was pierced by a blow that struck the
heart. The murderer wrenched the weapon from
its cruel wound and turned upon the other slave,
who rose in terror to leap into the river. The
hand of Peshala was upon the poor creature as he
sprang, and before the cry that rose to the horror-
parted lips of the slave could be uttered, the knife
was plunged to the hilt in his breast. With
apparent unconcern, the Libyan threw the bodies
into the river, and then, with the help of Bariet,
made the smaller boat fast to the barge, and
ordered the rowers to resume their places.

Exhausted by fear, and not fully appreciating
the danger in which she was placed, Abigail had
fallen asleep, and was spared the sight of this
horror. Elisheba, however, had not closed her

eyes, and when she observed the approach to another boat, she was for the moment buoyed with the hope that its occupants might discover that Abigail and herself were held as prisoners. She knew that the laws of the Egyptians were most considerate of women, and that the crime of abduction was punishable by death. Furthermore, whosoever might be cognizant of the commission of crime, and made no endeavor to prevent it, was held equally responsible with the perpetrator. It might be expected, therefore, that should captives be discovered in a boat upon the Nile, that great, free, open highway for all classes, account and explanation would be demanded of the captors, and in the absence of authority that might not be disputed, it would be the plain duty of the challengers to apprehend those who were under suspicion.

But how short-lived was this hope! In the faint light, Elisheba saw the few hideous details of the double tragedy, and her quick ears supplied whatever was mercifully hidden from her sight. The great depth of the villainy of this man who had seized upon her was now revealed in its most fearful form, and her gentle nature was so horrified that she sank into a swoon.

How long Elisheba remained in this state, she did not know, but she was aroused from unconsciousness by an inquiry from the slave as to their destination.

"To Manhotef, before dawn," was the reply, "and the time is short. Bend to your work, and I will double that which you expect as your share of the reward."

CHAPTER X

DRIFTING

RAMESES, where Meneptah held court, was a day's journey westward from Zoan by the eastern branch of the Nile. Manhotef, the point toward which Peshala was conveying his captives, was distant from Zoan about six hours. It had been a splendid city, reared under former dynasties, upon which the ever-shifting rivers of the delta had encroached until its habitations and temples were thrown down and in ruins. Then, when the ruin was complete, as if content with its work, the water again changed its course, and left the sorry monument of its power lying desolate and alone. In time, a few poor huts were raised out of the debris, and came to be occupied by criminals and outcasts from the populous towns, or by slaves who escaped from their masters, and in this labyrinth found hiding-places. Because of its isolation and reputation, the ruins of Manhotef would well serve the purpose of Peshala. Here he could find those who, for pay, would do his bidding and ask no questions. Indeed, he had previously made several visits to this desolate region with that end in view, and had formed acquaintances there upon whom he could depend for assistance in any nefarious scheme he might propose.

The ruined place was a considerable distance from the channel of the river, and was reached by passing over a low, flat shore, built up by the sluggish waters, which are ever bringing sediment from the thousand leagues of valley through which they flow. A luxuriant growth of papyrus, wild cane, and rushes covered this low and marshy plain, with narrow and winding paths leading through the tangle to the ruined city.

As the barge drew near Manhotef, Peshala bade the rowers cease their labor, and when they floated into the shallow water, he stepped out and waded to the higher ground. After a brief examination, he returned and guided the barge into a small pond, or lagoon, separated from the river by a sandy bar, along which grew a screen of water plants. With little effort the barge was forced over this bar, and once in the lagoon, it found a harbor that was almost entirely concealed from the river. It was now nearing dawn, and Bariet and the dwarf, who had been rowing steadily for hours, were greatly fatigued by their exertions. Peshala appeared to require neither food nor rest. He constantly paced the narrow barge, pausing at intervals to listen to the gentle breathing of his prisoners, who were covered with pieces of sail-cloth, and appeared to be sleeping. The wounds upon his face gave him considerable pain, and he had fears that the sight of his injured eye was destroyed. Each twinge was salved with the thought that he would visit months of in-dignity upon the girl who had caused his hurts, and for every mar upon his features he would see that the scourgers of the Pharaoh laid ten lashes upon the back of the man she loved.

As soon as the barge was moored, Peshala commenced preparations for the continuation of his journey to Rameses, which he desired to reach at an early hour, in furtherance of his designs to incite the wrath of Meneptah against the adon and his visitors. Threatened uprisings were ever dealt with promptly, and the Libyan entertained

little doubt that with the assistance of the ab he
could bring about the early dispatch of a considerable force. When this was done, and while
awaiting the return of the expedition, he would
make known to the ab his hopes as to reward, in
payment for his fidelity to the crown. In the
meantime, Bariet and the dwarf must remain
closely within the lagoon with the prisoners.
Here they would probably be safe from searching
parties, for Peshala argued that with the arrest of
Martiesen, the friend of the Hebrews, it would be
several days before the people of Zoan would find
it possible to get the authorities to act, and thus
his connection with the abduction would not be
known until he had fortified himself against
prosecution. They might expect to be visited by
beggars from Manhotef, who were to be silenced
with money, which he gave to Bariet in generous
quantity. Should a certain priest named Totoes
appear, he was to be told to await the return of
Peshala, before taking further steps in a matter
understood between them. Finally, if danger of
discovery arose from outside, they were to take
the captives to the ruins, which might be reached
by following any of the paths near them. Here
they would be concealed under the direction of

the priest until his return.

While he was imparting these instructions, the supplies were taken from the smaller boat, and placed upon the barge. Peshala took his seat in the light craft, the papyrus bushes on the sand bar were parted, and he struck rapidly out upon his journey. A dozen boat lengths from the hiding-place were not passed by the Libyan before there came over Egypt that strange darkness sent by the God of the Hebrews. Away in the east the stars were just beginning to pale before the glow of the advancing sun, when it came, and in a moment they were blotted out by the black and over-shadowing pall.

Peshala believed at first that he was stricken blind. He placed his hands upon his bandaged face a moment, but when he attempted again to see, he could discern nothing. The shape of his boat, the gleam of the water, a point of light, or even the faintest outline of the distant horizon would have given him courage; but these he sought in vain. He cursed Elisheba with the most fearful maledictions, and called upon all the gods in Libya and Egypt to come to his aid and assist in her punishment; he beat his hands upon the sides of the boat, and then dipped them in the river

and brought water to his face, to wash away the
veil that shut out his vision. Then he seized the
oars, and attempted to return to the lagoon; but
he was confused and baffled by the darkness, and
he could discover no approach to land. Re-
peatedly he shouted to Bariet, to come to his aid
or to guide him by his voice, and, thinking he
heard an answering cry, he rowed in desperation
in the direction whence it came; then paused and
cried again in alarm for help. The mocking echo
which first deceived him this time answered from
another quarter.

Rowing with desperation until nearly exhausted, sometimes bending over the side of his
boat and dipping water upon his heated face and
body, always straining his gaze and turning in
each direction in search of light, Peshala went
over the Nile, he knew not whither. Occasionally
his boat struck against a bank, and he reached out
to grope with his hands among the weeds and
sedges, or to wound his fingers upon the jagged rocks. At length — he could not reckon how
long a time since his start — he saw the dull glow
of a fire upon the shore, and then he knew he
was not blind. He paused, and to his ears came
the chanting of a priest and the moaning of

frightened men and women. He called loudly to the landing-place and begged assistance; but the cowering wretches thought evil spirits were speaking from the darkness, and they hurled clubs and stones toward him, and shouted to him to keep off. He rowed back as a matter of precaution, designing to land quietly, if possible, and join himself to the others, from whom he could at least receive companionship; and then he lost the faint glow of the fire, and was again by himself. However, this incident brought a grain of satisfaction. He was not blind, nor was it a fearful, haunting nightmare of insanity, as he so often dreaded. Other human beings were plunged in the same abyss, from which the stars, the sun, and every object or substance that could give light or radiation had disappeared. The calamity was a common one, and was not an affliction or punishment sent by the gods upon him alone. He decided that when next he came to land, he would leave the boat, and crawl along the shore, in the hope of discovering some being with whom he could converse. The solitude into which he was plunged was so overpowering that he felt as one upon the earth alone, and he longed for the touch of a hand or the sound of a voice in

sympathy. This thought gave birth to another:
What if he should come upon the bodies of the
slaves so unnecessarily murdered by his hand a
few hours before? With guilty fear he peered
from side to side upon the water, half expecting
to see the ghastly corpses floating before him.
Then he stood upright in the boat, with one of
the oars raised above his head, ready to strike,
and shouted to the dead to keep off, and declared
that Bariet and the dwarf gave the fatal blows
without his authority.

At length Peshala grew calmer, and when his
hands came in contact with some rice cakes
unintentionally left in one end of the boat, he
broke the food, and ate ravenously. In time he
slept, then awoke again, and rowed with vigor, he
knew not whither, until again exhausted with the
effort. His senses grew dull and sodden, and his
mind worked in a circle, as though drunken with
some benumbing drug. He heard the wailing
populace of a town, or the strange and piteous
cries of beasts, or saw the faint glimmer of the
fires; but neither the sounds nor the feeble lights
aroused in him curiosity, interest, or hope.
Stupefied, and at last incapable of action, the
Libyan sat with his hands resting upon the oars,

and drifted whither the river willed.

A cry — near and at one side of the boat — which might have been made by a bewildered waterfowl, an evil spirit, or an avenging fate, did not arouse him. A splash in the water, at his very keel, which sent a shower of spray over his body, failed to shake him from the lethargy in which he sat. A hand, grasping the boat's prow a long time, and then a body, slowly and cautiously rising, not seen, but felt through the tremor imparted to the craft, still failed to start one quickening thought in Peshala. The deep, labored breathing of a man resting from exertion and then the wary advance along the bottom of the boat, and the touch of a hand against his foot, but drawn hastily back, and then the hand again upon his knees, came to this living, yet lifeless boatman as half-realized actualities mingle with the mysteries of a troubled dream.

A voice: "Succor, my brother, I pray you, succor from my peril!"

And Peshala leaped to his feet, his nerves electrified, his body swaying with passion, his whole being awakened as completely as though the brilliance of noonday had burst through the pall of darkness.

"Who pleads for succor?" he shrieked in a voice from which every natural tone had departed.

"Martiesen, adon of the Nome of the Prince."

With a vehemence that was overpowering, the maddened Libyan leaped upon the half-prostrate body of his master. In the struggle that followed, the frail craft rocked and trembled as though it would split asunder or overturn. One knew the man with whom he fought and strove for mastery; the other, believing that he had to deal with some poor creature whose reason was unseated by the unreal conditions surrounding him, acted solely in defense. The contest was brief, for in a few minutes the strong, wiry hands of Peshala met upon the adon's throat with a grip that could not be shaken off. Back upon the bottom of the boat the secretary forced his victim, and held him thus with ever-tightening fingers until the adon's body grew limp and almost pulseless. Tearing his clothing into strips, Peshala bound Martiesen's hands and feet, and when this was accomplished, the panting, sweating, triumph-maddened victor rose to his full height above the pinioned, senseless body of his former master, and extending both arms above his head, laughed with the ecstasy of a fiend incarnate.

Hours, days, weeks, or seasons might have passed for aught either inmate of this drifting boat knew of the lapse of time. When Martiesen finally recovered consciousness, he realized that his companion was rowing as though life itself depended upon each stroke. After a time the rowing ceased, and the adon heard the oarsman muttering oaths against the gods, and with the next breath praising them. Martiesen did not as yet know his captor, nor could he explain why he was bound and held a prisoner. Remembering that his voice was the signal for the attack upon him, he feigned sleep, and gave no sign of consciousness. He felt the Libyan's hand upon his heart, seeking to know if life remained within the body of his prisoner, and then each knotted bond was tested by the same hot, feverish touch, which almost scorched the adon's flesh.

"Safe," he whispered in his native tongue, "safe for the vengeance that has been long in coming. Ah, my father, thy murderer is at the feet of thy son!"

"Peshala!"

The adon knew his captor now. He would burst the cords which held him; he would struggle with the man that had taken Elisheba from her home

— Elisheba whom Martiesen loved — and he would hurl him from the boat, and drag him down to the bed of the Nile.

But the struggle was in vain, for the Libyan threw himself upon the helpless adon, and held him with a force that could not be combated.

"Aye, you Egyptian dog! Peshala has you safe — Peshala who has sworn by all the souls of the Libyan dead that he would have revenge upon the slayer of his father."

"I have slain none save in open battle. Martiesen is not a murderer," replied the adon, with firmness.

"But it was your hand that brought my father to his death, and at the knees of the widowed mother his sons swore vengeance upon the slayer," hissed Peshala. "Two failed in their mission, and died like common captives under the slave-drivers in the Egyptian mines. The third, the last, will fulfill the oath."

"Who was your father? I know him not, nor do I know when I slew him."

The grip of Peshala tightened, and his knee pressed more firmly upon the adon's breast. "My father was the Libyan prince of whose conquest and death you boasted to me, his son. There in the salon you told me the story of my father's death, and before my eyes you displayed the royal heirloom taken from his dead and mutilated body, the priceless dagger which, in three centuries, was not touched by other than a royal hand."

"Then strike, if you be his son, strike and become a murderer! The Libyan prince was a powerful warrior, yet I, a mere stripling, conquered and slew him in battle. I cut him down as though he were a branch of papyrus growing in my path, and his soul went out rejoicing with the souls of others slain in battle. Strike, here in the darkness where the gods themselves cannot see the deed, and carry to your father, who sits with them, the story of your cowardice. You need not fear me now, for I am helpless, bound hand and foot, a fit victim for one who has become an abductor of defenseless women. Strike, Peshala, for no eye can look upon you!"

"Not yet, Martiesen, not yet will I strike. You may not escape so easily. For what is death to that which is in store? Your life is forfeit to the king, and he may have it when I have done with you. But when you stand before him in the judgment hall at Rameses, to answer to the charge of usurpation, it will strengthen your limbs and add courage to your heart, if you have seen Elisheba as the bondwoman of Peshala."

All the passion, the strength, the frenzy that possessed Martiesen when he first learned at Zoan that Elisheba was in the power of Peshala, returned in this instant, and with a desperation that threatened his dissolution, he struggled to free himself. Pinioned, and in the grasp of one wrought upon by hatred and the thirst for revenge, the adon's attempts were futile, but not until incapable of further effort by exhaustion did he cease to strive for freedom.

In time Peshala gave his prisoner some crumbs from the rice cakes, and freed one of his hands a moment to enable him to dip from the river and drink. Few words were spoken, for each read the thoughts of the other's heart, and remained silent. The Libyan now sought to avoid the shore, for whenever the boat touched upon a shelving beach, or struck against a perpendicular bank, he would turn in another direction, and row rapidly away. At intervals the adon slept, but woke often, ever to find that his captor was watchful and sleepless. When the prisoner moved to ease his bound and numbed limbs, he instantly felt the hands of Peshala passing rapidly over him to discover the condition of the knots by which he was fettered.

As the long night progressed, the Libyan grew more restless. He constantly uttered fearful curses upon the darkness, or prayed for a few hours of light in which to complete his revenge. Finally he leaned over the adon, and asked if he would not like to know where Elisheba and Abigail were concealed.

"I do not ask, for I do not expect the answer to be truthful. They are as safe from you now as though in their own home, that gives me contentment"

"Nay, but I have them safeguarded by Bariet and the dwarf, who will not play me false. I shall come upon them in the light, and you shall see — yes, you shall see."

"But the light! There may be no light, and then what of your plans? The God who sent this darkness can protect these Hebrew women, for in their homes there is light, as I saw with my own eyes, and outside their doors all is as black as the heart of Peshala."

"Whence came this night without an end?"

"From the God of the Hebrews, as a plague

upon Egypt's king and evil-doers. When that God commands, it will vanish; but how long it remains is not known."

"Curse the Hebrew God! He is greater than the gods of Egypt, but the gods of Libya are greater than all. To them will I pray that they dispel this gloom. I will offer them a sacrifice, a living Egyptian, torn and broken by anguish and pain, until he deserts all other gods and calls upon them for mercy. Curse the Hebrew God! Curse the Egyptian gods!"

He crept back to the oars, and Martiesen heard him offering incoherent prayers to the deities of his childhood.

Drifting for hours, and for other hours propelled by the oars of the baffled captor; backwards and forwards over the bosom of the black Nile, with the sluggish current, or against it; on, on, through the terrible Egyptian night, till reason trembled in the balance, and neither bound nor free realized the presence of the other!

CHAPTER XI

LIGHT IN DARKNESS

THE shouts of Peshala for assistance, when he was overtaken by the ninth plague sent by God upon the Egyptians, were heard within the lagoon. The dwarf shuddered in terror, for the cries were those of a man in distress, and apparently came from near at hand.

"Make no reply, Maesis," said Bariet. "We will forget that we have heard."

"But if the master returns, his anger will be spent upon us, if we fail to aid him."

"If he returns, we will be asleep in the barge, and declare that we heard nothing. He is not so sure of returning, for if he can see no more than I, he will have little chance of entering this small cove."

"Why should it be so dark, Bariet? I cannot see

the shape of my hands."

"A fog has drifted in from the great salt waters that are ever drinking up the Nile, and it may last for some hours. When it rises, we must escape from Peshala."

"What need is there of that? Have we not deserted our master, who was ever kind, to follow this terrible scribe? How may we now turn back?"

"Maesis, did you not see the murder of our fellow-slaves, Nilos and Stephen?"

"Aye, that I did, and my blood chilled at the sight."

"What reason was there for this murder, Maesis? Could he not have brought the slaves with him and set them free, or sold them to another? Yes, but that would not have satisfied his cruelty; and since he struck those blows, I have thought that we shall be dealt with in the same manner, when we have served his purpose."

"Hark! The gods defend us! He calls again."

"Yes," said Bariet, listening to the despairing cry, "but now he is more distant, and we need have no fear that he will find his way back. We shall do well if we ourselves reach the barge."

Hand in hand they groped slowly through the shallow water, until they finally came upon the boat, and entering the small cockpit under the pavilion, they lay down on the benches. "What will you do with the women, Bariet, these that he has stolen?" asked the dwarf.

"We have no means of escape except by the barge," replied the Assyrian. "This is a place where there are many murderers and runaway slaves, and if we fall into their hands, they will deliver us to Peshala immediately upon his return. We must go by the river, and the Hebrew girls will go with us."

"No, Bariet, you are not so cunning as I thought. It will not do to return them to their homes, for in doing so we should be captured by the adon, and he would execute us for our part in this night's work. We must leave them here."

"That would be a monstrous thing to do, Maesis; for what would befall them in Manhotef, where none but criminals lurk? Besides, if we return them to the Hebrews uninjured, they will plead for us, and we shall be rewarded for returning them to freedom. Leave it to me, for I see our way clear — if only the fog would lift — to turn the circumstances to our account."

The dwarf did not reply, and soon fell asleep. The Assyrian watched patiently, but as the hours lengthened, his vigil relaxed, and he, too, sank into slumber.

When Elisheba and Abigail awoke, and found themselves in darkness, they were content to remain hidden in its folds as long as danger was not apparent. They heard the deep breathing of the slaves, and, whispering softly to each other, wondered at the length of the night. After a long time Elisheba succeeded in freeing her hands, and when she recovered their use, she loosened the bonds upon Abigail and herself. With the hope of escape, she crept carefully about the barge, and after listening intently from every point she could approach, arrived at the conclusion that Peshala was not present. She came upon food and jars of wine, and when she had conveyed a generous portion to the pavilion, the sisters ate with relish, and in hushed voices discussed how they might elude their captors. If they could only reach the open bank of the river, they thought it might be possible to attract the attention of boatmen with signals, and in this manner make known their plight. Thus planning, plotting, wondering, whispering love and encouragement to each other, fearing for the anxiety and sorrow of their father when he should learn that they had not been taken to the home of the adon, as he expected, and then wondering again, ever wondering at the almost stifling darkness, the sisters waited for the coming of light.

At length the dwarf awoke, and finding only darkness, called in terror to Bariet.

"Why, what is this, Maesis? Not yet light?" said the Assyrian in deep alarm.

"No, Bariet, though I have slept long, it is still as dark as when we returned to the boat."

"Indeed you slept long, for I sat beside you until I was numb, waiting for a sight of the shore, and finally I, too, fell asleep."

"What can it mean? I have never seen darkness like this," said the dwarf, drawing back from the entrance. "Once at my home in Ethiopia the sun was darkened for a time by a black shadow which swept across its face, but the light soon returned."

"That was a portent of war."

"Indeed it was, for in a few days the Egyptians came, and many of our people were slain, and I was driven from my home with many other captives."

"One who has been a captive can never lose from his heart all pity for other captives. Maesis, will you stand with me in the attempt to return

Elisheba and Abigail to their home?"

"Bariet, I will follow your lead."

"Maesis, are you armed?"

"Only with the knife in my girdle."

"Then we will not permit Peshala to come again upon the barge, should he return. And from this time on one of us must watch for the breaking of light, while the other sleeps. We must escape him if it be possible, for if the murderer of our companions finds us in this place, and we resist, he will summon help from the ruins, and overpower us."

Elisheba heard their voices, and creeping to the edge of the platform, asked of what they were speaking.

"Of the darkness, my lady, for the time of morning has long since passed."

"Where is Peshala?"

"He departed in the small boat for Rameses before the hour of dawn."

The hearts of the sisters leaped with great joy.

"And did the deeper darkness come after he left?" asked Elisheba, when she could control her voice.

"Immediately, my lady. Peshala was not a score of boat lengths upon the river when the black fog swept down, and in an instant we could see nothing. It was with difficulty that we returned to the barge from the entrance to the cove after we had sped Peshala on his journey."

"Surely he must have become confused and lost his way, or he would have returned ere this," said the girl.

"Indeed, lady, he was blinded from the start, for we heard his cries for aid, but did not answer them."

"You did not reply to them, Bariet?"

"No, lady, we stopped both our ears and our mouths after his first shouts."

Was there cause for hope or for fear in this action of the slaves? "Bariet, why did you refuse to answer Peshala or assist him to return?"

"I have feared him since he stabbed the slaves, our companions," replied the Assyrian, truthfully, "and have sought occasion for escape."

"Then fear him no longer," said Elisheba. An inspiration came to her with the reply of Bariet. Her eyes were opened, and she saw that the hand of God was stretched forth to aid her people.

"The darkness was sent as another plague upon the Egyptians," she said. "Peshala wanders in it upon the Nile, and it will hold him, and baffle

him, and beat him down in his evil designs upon
your master and myself. He will neither come
upon Rameses, nor the place where we lie, nor
any place of shelter. His evil thoughts and passions will drive him to madness."

Bariet shook with terror, for Elisheba, speaking
out of the darkness, was more like a disembodied
spirit than a living person. The dwarf clung to the
Assyrian's limbs with trembling hands.

She waited a moment before she spoke again,
"Bariet, surely you have no cause to injure the
Hebrew Darda."

"None, my lady."

"Nor have you enmity against my sister and
myself, for we have not harmed you."

"It is true, Elisheba; I have not."

"Then why should you hold us here as
prisoners for the man you so greatly fear? Return
us to our home, Bariet, and you shall be pro-
tected from Peshala."

"Lady, even before you spoke to us, Maesis
entered into a compact with me that we should
do as you have asked. We shall return to our
master and ask his forgiveness, but first the
Hebrew maidens shall be restored to their
father."

"O Bariet, if you and the dwarf will be faithful in this, I will entreat the adon for your freedom as a reward."

"Faithful, my lady Elisheba! I swear by all the gods of Assyria and Egypt, nay, by the God of the Hebrews I swear it, Bariet will be faithful, and the dwarf will be faithful to the end. And for reward, we ask it not."

The earnestness of the slave's voice gave assurance that he would do as he promised, for there was no doubt that he was now fully enlisted in the cause. At intervals in the long hours of waiting she talked to the slaves from the pavilion, sustaining their hope and winning their sympathies by her gentle and kindly interest in their welfare. Occasionally the faith of the sisters wavered, and they feared, they knew not what. But then arose the promises of the prophets to comfort them, and the remembrance that heretofore all had been fulfilled, and with these thoughts trust and confidence returned, and they awaited the end with patience.

On the morning of the fourth day the faint glow of the coming sun burned in the heavens to herald the passage of the long night, and with the first almost imperceptible touch of the morning, a thrill of joy ran through the hearts of despairing men. Beasts, too, and fowls arose from places where they had fallen, while stunted vegetation, grown pale and sickly by the withdrawal of that which gives it life, once more lifted its leaves and spires and drooping blossoms, and fluttered gaily in the reawakening light.

Elisheba, watchful and restless, became aware of the breaking of the morning, when she saw dim outlines of the papyrus rushes near the barge. She leaped to her feet, filled with breathless joy, but half fearing at first that she was deceived. Ah, no, there was light, the blessed light, and upon its wings it bore the hope of freedom! With quick and loving caresses she awakened Abigail, and as they gazed first upon each other's features, and then there in the east upon the coming glory, they felt their hearts bursting with the knowledge that the God of the Hebrews still lived.

Running to the sleeping men, Elisheba shook Bariet by the shoulder, and called to him:

"Awake! awake! Bariet, awake, for the light is here to set us free! Quick, Maesis, quick to the oars," and she turned to the dwarf, "for the morning comes, and we can hasten from this place. Look, Bariet, the promise of the Assyrian slave can now be kept."

The men sprang to their feet, thrilled with the joy of her voice. Yes, here was light! O wonder that it had come at last! And there was none at hand to stay them. They danced upon the swaying boat, chanting, each in his mother tongue, their simple thanksgiving. Then, with uplifted faces, extended arms, and bared breasts, they waited, as though to catch and hold and never lose the subtle, mysterious gift that is life itself.

"Quick, quick, Bariet, Maesis, to the oars and to the river!" urged the impatient girl "We are free to go now, but should we delay till Peshala returns, all is lost."

The slaves leaped to obey her commands, for the name of the Libyan stirred them to a recollection of their danger. As they sprang toward the oars, a tall, half-clad figure ran through the shallow water from the nearby shore and laid his hand upon the prow of the barge.

"Why in such haste to leave fair and beautiful Manhotef?" he demanded.

It was Totoes, the outcast priest. He had found an asylum in this desolate place some years previously, and was thus able to escape punishment for a number of atrocious crimes in which he had been detected.

"We return to Zoan," replied Elisheba, with courage on her lips but fear in her heart. "We have been compelled to remain here because of the darkness, and we fear that our friends will be sorely distressed over our absence."

"Hebrews!" said Totoes, with contempt. "If your friends are anxious over this short delay, they may be even more concerned should it be extended, and thus be induced to place a ransom on your pretty heads."

Then, glancing over the barge in the twilight, he demanded the name of its owner.

"Martiesen, adon of the Nome of the Prince," answered Bariet with spirit, "and we be his slaves. Stand you aside and permit its departure." He arose from the rower's seat and approached the priest.

"So, it is Bariet, of whom Peshala has told me something," replied Totoes. "This furnishes a still more urgent reason why you should remain, for unless I mistake, you came hither on some business of your master's secretary. It appears to me rather dangerous to permit two handsome maidens to go abroad at the mercy of a couple of desperate slaves, therefore I urge you to dis-embark immediately, and accompany me to a place which will not be so easy of discovery when the day breaks fully. Martiesen may be search-ing for his slaves."

Abigail touched Elisheba's arm and motioned to the water. Bariet detected the movement, and in a glance his quick eye saw four gaunt, hollow-eyed figures cautiously approaching the boat. They had stolen into the lagoon, and had all but reached the barge without detection, while Totoes parleyed with its occupants.

With a cry of warning to the dwarf, Bariet leaped forward upon the priest, who scarcely anticipated resistance, and bore him down into the shallow water. After dealing the struggling Totoes a blow which stunned him into insen-sibility, Bariet braced his shoulder against the prow of the barge, and with a mighty effort freed it from the soft mud into which it had settled. He caught the prow with his single hand, and attempted to swing himself upon the barge, but at that instant there was the gleam of a knife in the air, for one of the priest's followers who had gained the barge leaned over the side, and struck viciously at the slave. Bariet dodged the blow,

and down beside him fell a dark body with a
great, gaping wound in its back, which had been
made by the knife of the dwarf. A scream from
Elisheba caused Bariet to redouble his efforts to
regain the deck of the boat, and when in a
moment he succeeded, he sprang over the prostrate, struggling bodies of the dwarf and an
antagonist, and reached the pavilion in a bound.
There, in the grasp of one of the ruffians, who
held the girl in front of him as a shield, Bariet saw
the tender and unconscious form of Abigail.
Like a tigress aroused to the protection of her
young, Elisheba was advancing upon the
Egyptian, yet dared not strike with the dagger she
held, fearing that the blow would reach her sister
first. Nor did she dare delay, for the Egyptian
crept back inch by inch, feeling with outstretched
foot for the edge of the platform, ready when he
should reach it to leap backwards into the water
with his victim, and then bear her away captive.
With the rapidity of thought, Bariet caught a
throw-stick from his belt, and hurled it across the
pavilion, crashing into the skull of Abigail's
captor. He followed his weapon with a bound.
The stricken man toppled over the barge into the
lagoon, still clasping the unconscious child in his

arms. Without an instant's hesitation, Bariet leaped again into the water. He was up to his armpits now, but with unerring instinct he sank to the bottom of the pond, and in a moment brought the pale, white form of the girl from the grasp of the swarthy corpse that held it in a death's embrace. Bearing her up as best he could, Bariet raised the child to the agonized sister, whose trembling arms reached eagerly down for the precious burden.

But Bariet knew that his task was not finished. The fifth of their assailants had gone to the assistance of Totoes, and, after dragging the stunned priest to the shore, shouted loudly for aid. Answering cries were heard in the distance, and the crashing of dry reeds and papyrus along the narrow paths warned the slave that followers of Totoes would soon overpower him, and the escape of those for whom he was fighting with so much courage would be impossible.

"To the oars, Elisheba!" he shouted. "To the oars, with all your strength."

He seized the prow of the boat, and pointed it toward the river, now plainly visible in the increasing light. Wading where he could, swimming where the water was too deep for him to walk upon the bottom, he put his shoulder against the stern of the barge and pressed forward to freedom. Elisheba heard Bariet's cry, and threw all her strength upon the oars, thus greatly aiding the almost superhuman efforts of the slave who was striving to save them. Together they succeeded, and as they passed over the bar upon which grew the fringe of papyrus screening the lagoon from the river, a crowd of desperate wretches burst upon the shores of the harbor just quitted, and plunged into the water as if to follow the escaping barge. By this time Bariet was upon the boat, and after pausing long enough to raise a pulseless body from the feeble grasp of Maesis and fling it overboard, he caught the oars from Elisheba's hands, and with long sweeps sent the craft out of the shadow, upon the broad bosom of the sparkling Nile.

By and by Elisheba came running to him, all radiant with hope and happiness.

"She lives!" the girl cried in answer to his wondering look. "She lives, Bariet, and we shall restore her to her father's loving arms. O Bariet, noble Bariet, what reward is great enough to compensate you for the happiness you have brought to others!"

Into the worn and exhausted countenance of the slave came a glow of satisfaction and content. He had done the work according to his pledge, and he felt the reward of well-doing in his heart. As well as she could, Elisheba washed and bound the wounds of the unconscious dwarf, who had fought against a powerful man, and was dangerously hurt. With tenderness she placed his body in a comfortable position, and shielded him from the sun. Keeping well towards the western shore, Bariet toiled steadily at the oars. The barge was a heavy craft for two rowers, and with but one its progress was slow and laborious. Nevertheless, Bariet was determined to succeed, for he had enlisted in this cause with his whole soul, and would make the fight as long as there was life in his body. The stump of his maimed arm, bent over the oar handle, was not as effectual as the grasp of a hand. Because it often gave him trouble, he asked Elisheba to bring a band and fasten his arm to the oar; but she came with compassion in her face, and, seizing the oar with her own hands, took her place beside the slave, and kept the stroke. Bariet protested that it was not fit work for her, and declared that he could row the entire distance to Zoan, if she would bind his arm to the oar. She shook her head till all her glittering wealth of hair fell down over her neck and shoulders, and kept her place.

"No, Bariet, I will stay. You have saved us from a fate many times more dreadful than death, and are striving to complete our escape. You have lost sight of yourself, and are thinking only of aiding two helpless women of another race. Bariet, I am proud to sit here beside you, and do what I may to help."

About midday they passed the adon's villa, far to the right. Bariet asked if they should land and seek aid; but Elisheba, fearing her father's great anxiety, begged that they incur no delay. And so, with Abigail coming often to them with refreshment, and sometimes singing pretty, childish songs to cheer them on, they toiled steadily forward.

CHAPTER XII

OTHER CAPTIVES

MARTIESEN opened his eyes upon the returning light, and saw sitting before him in the boat, with listless hands and head bent forward on sunken breast, in stupor like that of apoplectic seizure, the helpless Peshala. The Libyan's face was covered with patches of dried blood, two livid scars were upon his cheeks, and one eye was torn, lacerated, and swollen with inflammation — a revolting, sickening object.

They had been without food two days and two nights, and the day and night preceding that period they had partaken only of a few small pieces of rice cakes. Both labored under the stress of consuming passion, followed by the outlay of most unusual exertion and exhausting strife. The environments were of that character which drive men to madness or impel them to self-destruction. Though each was worn to the verge of physical and mental collapse, Martiesen was the stronger, for his strength had not been weakened and sapped by the continual brooding upon and thirst for vengeance, as was the case with Peshala. Not only was the Libyan worn and mentally enervated by these influences, but he had now been rowing the boat at intervals for three days and nights. Sometimes he would work at the oars for hours without pausing, and possibly in all that time accomplish little more than a circle or a zigzag course upon the river.

The adon gazed dreamily and wonderingly at his captor in the growing light. He could make nothing out of the situation at first — his bound feet and hands, his aching head and body, his torn and soiled clothing, himself there at the bottom of the boat, and the swaying, stupefied figure before him — it was all mystery. Only by slow degrees did it come back to Martiesen, that horrible nightmare through which he had passed. For a time he continued to think it a hideous dream, and he endeavored to shake it off. But as he strove to awaken to something else, he lost himself, and in place of reality came a vision of a fete where there were sparkling lights and flash-ing gems, tinkling harps and dancing maidens, and Elisheba by his side. He bent his head to speak to her, and when she turned to answer his inquiry, the evil face of Peshala swam before his eyes.

Then the adon awoke, and in the clearer light he saw and realized all. The boat was drifting near a bank, a barren, rocky, desolate spot, and no habitation was within view.

"Arouse! arouse!" he called to Peshala. "The light has come, and it is now the hour to com-plete your work."

The secretary half raised his head, and sank again in stupor.

"Awake, Peshala! It is Martiesen who speaks, the hated adon, upon whom you may now have vengeance!"

He thought the man was dying there before him, and feared that ere help came, he, too, might die, bound as he was and powerless to rise. He raved, shouted, and rocked the boat by rolling from side to side; but his cries fell upon un-heeding ears, and the swaying figure gave no sign of intelligence.

Turning his head, Martiesen caught sight of a

knife that had been lost in the boat by one of the murdered slaves, and had not been found by Peshala. Inch by inch he wormed his body over to the weapon, until his hands, tied behind his back, could touch the blade. His nerveless fingers failed again and again to set the knife upright, where he could press the bands of cloth that held his wrists against the keen edge; but at length he succeeded, and he felt the blood tingling through the clogged veins of his hands. Hope was born anew with this achievement, and when Martiesen had beaten his numb hands and arms upon his body until their use was possible, he grasped the knife, and freed his limbs. This done, he leaned over the boat, and dipping up water in his palms from the Nile, he slaked his thirst, and bathed his head and face in the refreshing element.

The adon's thoughts worked more readily now, and he realized that if he would discover where Peshala had secreted Elisheba and Abigail, he must act quickly; for the secretary sat there, making no sound and gazing fixedly at his feet, like a corpse propped to a sitting posture. Martiesen grasped the Libyan by his shoulders, and drew him backward to the bottom of the boat, and then dipping water from the river, threw it upon his face, and forced some of the liquid into his mouth. With all his strength he chafed the lifeless limbs and body, hoping to stimulate them into activity; but when he failed in this, he beat with the flat blade of the knife upon the soles of the Libyan's feet, or pricked his body with the point. Constantly he called:

"Arouse! arouse! Peshala! Here is Martiesen, your enemy. Come, awaken, and go to the Pharaoh to expose the plot to usurp the throne! Arouse! arouse!"

Then he would bend to the deaf ears and speak into them:

"Where are Elisheba and Abigail? In what place have you shut them with Bariet and the black dwarf on guard? Speak, Peshala, where is Elisheba?"

At length there was a convulsive working of the unconscious man's lips, and the lids closed over the sightless eyes. Thus encouraged, the adon renewed his efforts, and when he had labored faithfully for some minutes, he demanded again the place where Elisheba was secreted. There was an effort to rise, and then the Libyan sank back again with a faintly-whispered word upon his lips, but the eager man beside him caught as it escaped —

"Man-ho-tef!"

Rising from the body of the secretary, the adon searched the shores for a familiar landmark. He could not see distinctly, for his eyes swam with weakness, but he judged that the ruins of Manhotef lay a long distance below them. Summoning all his strength, he took the oars, and bent to the task of searching out the place. At first his strokes were slow and feeble, but in time they became more regular, and he was able to keep steadily upon his way. The sun was fully risen when he came upon a village, and from some of the people at the landing-place he purchased food and wine:

"Were you lost in the darkness, my master?" asked the man who supplied him, as Martiesen ravenously ate the cakes.

"Aye, with my companion here," was the adon's reply.

"Is the slave alive?"

"I think not by this time, for I have been unable to arouse him."

The villager bent over the boat, and examined the secretary. "He is near death," was his verdict, "but he may revive."

Then, moistening some of the bread with wine, the villager forced open the secretary's jaws, and placed a portion of the paste in his mouth.

"You are a nobleman?" said the villager, glancing at the empty dagger sheath at the adon's belt and clinking in his palms the silver rings that had been given to him for the food.

The adon bowed, and then, turning quickly to the man, asked him what he thought of the darkness, and whence it came.

"Osiris protect us!" exclaimed the man, and those who stood near him upon the bank called to their gods in fear.

"Indeed, it was terrible," continued the villager, "and many people died of fear, while others lost their reason."

"How long did it last?" inquired the adon.

"Do you not know, when you were upon the Nile through it all?"

"I lost the measure of time," Martiesen replied, "and whether it has been days or weeks, I do not know. I must have been unconscious some portion of the period, and my slave went mad before he became helpless."

"The darkness was upon us three days and nights," said the villager, in an awed tone, "and in that space our lamps and torches gave but a sickly glimmer that could not be distinguished more than a few paces off."

"But do you know whence it came?" persisted the adon.

"Nay, my master, ask me not, for it is a mystery not given the unlearned to know." The villager took a papyrus leaf, and, bending it in the form of a funnel, poured some of the wine between the Libyan's half-closed lips.

"The slave may live," he said, "for see, he has swallowed the wine."

"Which way lies Manhotef?" asked the adon with scarcely a glance at Peshala.

"Here, below, four leagues away. But you are not going to Manhotef, my master?"

"No? Why not?"

"Because it is peopled by outcasts and thieves, men who have fled to its ruins to escape the result of their crimes. It is a fearful place, and honest men, when passing, keep upon the other side of the Nile, as far from the Manhotef shore as possible."

"Yes, I have known its reputation long," responded the adon, "and you speak truly concerning it. Notwithstanding this, I go to

Manhotef, for there is work there for an honest man to do."

"My master, it is foolhardy, for unless you have soldiers at your back, you will not return thence alive."

"I thought to procure some of your stout young villagers, to accompany me in a larger boat," said the adon. "I can pay them well."

"Not for all the gems in the sheath of your dagger would one from this village risk his life at Manhotef. We have no military here, and our young men are few."

Martiesen looked upon the assembled peasants, but they shook their heads, and one and all timidly drew back.

"Then I shall go alone," he declared. "There is no time to wait for forces, which cannot be procured nearer than Rameses or the villa of the adon Martiesen."

"It is most dangerous, my master," insisted the villager.

"But there are now at Manhotef, if they be yet alive, those who may be in greater danger than that of death," said Martiesen. This thought urged upon him the necessity for haste, and he caught up the oars, and struck forward.

"Give the slave frequently of the wine," called the villager, "and he may recover to aid you."

"Perhaps it were better for him that he should die," was the adon's response.

The dried fish, cakes, and the wine, of which Martiesen partook freely, not only greatly refreshed and strengthened him, but banished from his soul every thought of fear. He fully realized the danger which he ran in attempting single-handed the rescue of Elisheba and Abigail; but to await assistance might mean death or dishonor for those he sought. He anticipated that ransom would be demanded, and this he was willing to pay for their release. Should he find, however, that harm had come to the daughters of the Hebrew, either from the slaves, in charge of whom he was almost certain they had been left, or from the outcasts who infested that shore, then he would seek that revenge which alone may wipe out such a stain; and first of all he would have vengeance upon the man at his feet, who was the primary cause of their misfortune. Then the adon remembered that he could not attack Peshala while he was insensible and helpless, for that would be cowardly assassination, a crime which he abhorred. So he frequently paused from his rowing to ply the man with wine, and before half the distance was covered, the secretary sat up in the boat and gazed wonderingly at his master. The adon placed the clumsy knife, which had served him so well in severing his bonds, in the sheath at his side, and knew that he now held a distinct advantage over the Libyan. After a time he spoke:

"Hear me, Peshala, for once more I am the master; do you know whither we go?"

The Libyan looked upon the shores, and shook his head.

"I will tell you then. We are nearing Manhotef."

Peshala started, and a flush came to his face, but he made no reply. Soon he took some of the food, and began to eat.

"You told me when scarcely life remained within you, that Elisheba and her sister were at Manhotef, and I have revived you for the purpose of taking you there. If we find these maidens safe, you may go and enjoy such pleasure in your life as your evil thoughts will give; but if harm has come to them, you shall be the first victim of my arm. Now pray to your gods that those whom you placed in such danger may have passed through it unscathed."

The adon rowed in silence after this, and with great rapidity, until he saw that they were nearing the point upon which the ruined city lay. As he approached the shore, he motioned to Peshala.

"Take the oars, and land where you left the barge," he said.

The secretary staggered into the rower's seat, and feebly grasped the oars. He searched the shore a moment as if in doubt, and then, pointing the boat to the thin line of bushes screening the lagoon, he moved the craft forward. They came to the mud bar, and Martiesen, bending over the prow, parted the reeds with his hands, and by pulling the tough branches assisted the boat into the harbor. Leaping to his feet, he swept the margin of the narrow pond with a quick glance, and then turned like a god of wrath upon the Libyan, and caught the trembling wretch by the throat with a grasp that meant death.

"False to the last," he growled, as he threw Peshala to the bottom of the boat, "but here your life of deception ends!"

Martiesen would delay no longer. He would crush this creature down, and tear his body to shreds, for in this moment there was in his heart neither pity nor quarter.

A dark form rose quickly from the bushes on the shore; a naked arm poised an instant in the air, then straight to the head of the adon, like the swift dart of a swallow, whirled a throw-stick.

The clenched fingers loosened their grip upon the insensible Peshala, and the adon, swaying a moment, like a man to whom death comes while yet he is standing upright, fell heavily forward upon his face.

"It was prettily done, Tarta," said Totoes, when the boat was brought to the shore. "In all my life I have never seen a better throw at such a distance. But I fear you were too strong, for the man dropped like a bull."

"Nay, he is not dead, unless he has a remarkably thin skull, for I threw a glancing blow," answered the villain called Tarta, as the priest and half a dozen others gathered around the boat. The priest looked on with interest, as the adon's body was turned to disclose his face.

"Martiesen, my lord adon!" he exclaimed. "And this is his scribe, as I live. Indeed this is a day of marvels. But how is it that this adon comes here with Peshala, and from the south at that? No doubt the visit has some relation to the presence here this morning of the adon's barge and the two fair prisoners. But why did the adon leap at the throat of his secretary, as though to rend him in tatters, as soon as they came into the harbor?"

Talking half-aloud and asking many questions, but answering none, Totoes carefully examined the insensible men.

"The lord adon will give us no trouble for several hours at least," he declared. "Tarta is a master hand, and had he been here when that cursed Bariet and his dwarf were slashing right and left, we should have made a handsome catch for one day. Peshala is harder used than the adon," he continued, "for he is even now on the verge of death.

"I don't think he is worth any trouble on our part. The adon is the one we want. He is rich, and his ransom must be his weight in gems, and gold, and silver. He must not die; but this carrion here may be sent adrift."

Totoes walked aside where he could plan his course without interruption. Upon his evil face, made more revolting by the blow dealt by Bariet, there was displayed cunning, avarice, and kindred base passions. He was a man of learning and intellectual power, and it was not strange that he had attained the leadership of the rogues at

Manhotef, and held them completely under his control. He feared no opposition to any plan he might propose, and when he solved, to his own satisfaction, the reason why the adon appeared there so soon after the return of light, he saw in the whole circumstance a more advantageous condition to himself than would have come about, had the plans of Peshala not miscarried.

Returning to the boat, he commanded Tarta and several others to convey Martiesen carefully to a certain mastaba, or underground tomb, near the gateway of a ruined temple, the entrance to which was so covered with broken columns and fallen walls that it could be discovered only by those who knew its location. As the men raised the adon from the boat, Totoes unclasped the belt from which hung the gem-covered sheath and a purse containing a quantity of gold and silver rings. He knew his followers too well to trust so much of value in their hands. Turning again to the boat, Totoes made another examination of the Libyan.

"He cannot live until evening," he declared. "Take the food and wine from the boat, for they are of more use here than with a man who cannot consume them, and then send the craft adrift in the river."

He watched the men as they executed his commands, and saw, without protest, that they stripped all articles of value from the body of the unconscious man. When this was done, one of the grinning wretches extended his hands towards the Libyan's throat and looked inquiringly at Totoes.

The priest shook his head. "No," he said, "let the gods take him. He will die soon enough." And he motioned towards the river.

Two of the men swam with the boat to the entrance of the lagoon, and then with all their strength thrust it far out in the stream, where it would be caught by the sluggish current and float away.

CHAPTER XIII

THE HOMECOMING

WHEN the plague of darkness passed from the land of Egypt, the tasks required of the Hebrews were not again taken up. So great was the fear of the Hebrew God and His mysterious and irresistible power, that outside the Pharaoh's own household and the temples of Isis and Osiris, where thousands of priests strove to retain their hold upon the superstitious masses, there could be found few with courage to execute the commands of the king or raise their hands against the Hebrews. All Egypt saw that to which the ruler was blind, and had Martiesen been at the capital of his nome, and set up his standard in revolt at that time, he could have succeeded to the throne without striking a serious blow. It was recognized that the Hebrews were under some peculiar

protection, and their great leader Moses was regarded with a feeling of undisguised awe.
Therefore, when it was known that the Pharaoh
had driven Moses from Rameses, with the warning that, should the prophet appear again at the
capital, he must die, the Egyptians sought to
evade the wrath which they expected to follow,
and vied with each other in extending kindness to
those upon whom their government laid such
heavy burdens.

Thus it was possible for the friends of Darda to
assemble at his home, unhampered by taskmasters, to mourn with the aged father for the
daughters who had been so unfairly decoyed
from his protection. The Libyan dagger carried
by Martiesen when he went forth on the mad
pursuit of Peshala after the secretary's perfidy was
made known to him, was found on the landing-
place, and the half-sunken boat which the adon
had accidentally destroyed as he swam in the
darkness, was discovered some distance down the
Nile.

There was small doubt in the minds of those
who searched that the adon had been drowned,
and messengers were dispatched along the river
in quest of his body, that it might be embalmed,

as became one of his rank.

A boat was procured, and preparations were in progress for Darda and Masarah to visit the villa, for the purpose of acquainting Panas and the princes with the fate that had overtaken Martiesen. It was also the intention of the Hebrew to plead that a force be sent to search for his absent daughters and visit punishment upon those who took them away. The Ethiopians were seated at the oars, and Masarah was about to embark, when she discovered, approaching in the distance, the barge bearing Elisheba, Abigail, Bariet, and the wounded dwarf. The soothsayer called to those at the landing, and inquired if the craft was not Martiesen's. Instantly all was commotion, for many came running to the wharf, wondering at what they saw. Soon they could make out a girlish figure standing in the bow, constantly waving her hands to those in whom hope was reawakened. And then this hope grew to conviction, and the sharpest of vision shouted, "It is Abigail!" and clasped their hands, and waved their open palms to heaven, and shouted yet again, "It is Abigail!"

Only to Darda there came no hope, for the old man feared it was a taunting vision that would vanish, and in departing leave him more hopeless than before it came. He lost courage to look, and, bowing himself to the earth, covered his head with his garment. The voices of his neighbors came to his ears, but he could not trust himself to listen, and so muffled his hearing with his hands, but from his heart there arose an appeal that the faint ray of courage which had sprung up therein might not be cut down.

The barge came steadily to the landing, while the shouts of welcome grew with every moment, but the father heard them only as a distant murmur. Elisheba, dropping the oar upon which she had toiled so steadily much of the day, took Abigail by the hand, and they ran together up the narrow steps. Pushing all aside, they hastened to the drooping, broken figure of the old man, and drew his garment from his face, and caught him in their arms, rained caresses on his cheeks, and spoke loving words into his ears. Then Darda knew that all was well, and clasping his dear ones to his heart, he raised his eyes to the smiling heavens, and poured forth thanks to that Being who had brought his daughters safe through every danger to their father's arms.

The details of the journey of the prisoners up the Nile, the departure of Peshala, the long night of waiting, the attack by Totoes and his followers, the peril of Abigail, the heroism of Bariet and Maesis, were quickly told to the old man and those who crowded to his side. Upon Bariet were lavished the grateful thanks of all, but the poor dwarf was beyond knowledge of their gratitude. He had grown feverish during the latter part of the journey, and though constantly ministered to by Abigail was rapidly sinking as they came to the wharf. He was conveyed to a comfortable place, and all the tenderness possessed by these primitive people was expended in his care, but he grew rapidly weaker, and soon expired.

Masarah gathered every circumstance of Elisheba's story, and was in haste to depart for the home of the adon. Though fearing that Martiesen was dead, she nevertheless, as is the fashion with womankind, and has been since the world began, held out to Elisheba every faint hope. But the maiden mourned her lover as one lost, and bending her head in silent grief sought solitude in her home. Mute from the weight of her sorrow, she sat apart on the earthen floor, neither seeing nor heeding the preparations round her. Finally Bariet came, and kneeling by her side spoke in a low voice:

"Lady, do not mourn the master as one who is dead, for he lives, and I will find him. I go with Masarah, and when we return, Martiesen will come with us."

"Nay, Bariet, it cannot be," she said slowly. "He was lost in the Nile the first night of the darkness, lost in his effort to save me from Peshala. They have told me all."

"Listen, Elisheba, for what I say is truth. As I rowed with all my strength to escape from Manhotef, while yet you were ministering to Abigail, and we were in danger from pursuit, I became faint with my exertions, and my soul was as if it had been taken from my body by the gods, and held suspended at a great height over the Nile. I could look upon our own barge, and see the river for a long distance up and down. I could see myself working at the oars, and I wondered at the strangeness of my vision; and I also saw that they had no boats at the lagoon, and were not following us. But far up the river I saw a boat, and — Elisheba, this I know to be true — Martiesen sat at the oars, while in the bottom of the boat, staring straight up as though dead, lay Peshala."

She caught his arm, and to her face came a startled, wondering look, which changed in a moment to doubt and unbelief.

"Impossible, Bariet! Why do you tell me this idle tale?"

"It is not idle, my lady. As plainly as you can see your father standing there with Abigail clinging to his side, I saw as I have told. And as I gazed in wonderment, you came running to that part of myself which was rowing there upon the barge, and cried out that Abigail lived. Your words called back to my body that which sees and knows, and which the gods held in their hands. Then I knew that it was a vision."

"But, Bariet, if you saw this, why did you toil so hard to put as many leagues as possible between us and Manhotef? Why did you not await the coming of the adon, and warn him of the danger that threatened, should he land where Peshala secreted us?"

"Had I told you of this at that time, my lady, you would have looked upon it as a poor plan to entrap you in a snare of my own, and you would not have given consent to a return to Manhotef or to a pause in our progress. Nor did I at the time believe that that which I had seen could be true, for I supposed my master at the villa or here at Zoan. When I returned, and they told me how the adon was lost in the river while searching for you, I knew that my vision had not lied."

Elisheba arose, and placed her hand on his arm.

"You have given me hope, Bariet, when a moment ago I was in deepest despair. I cannot explain why it is, or how this can be, but I will believe. Go, Bariet, make haste to tell Panas all you have told to me. Do not delay, for even now the adon may be a prisoner in the hands of those who sought our capture. I shall think of him as alive from this time; and may the God of my people protect him, until you will give him aid."

⌒IIII

CHAPTER XIV

DISGUISES

WITH a thousand hopes following in their train, Masarah and Bariet departed for the villa. It was Elisheba's desire to accompany them, but it was pointed out that her presence would in no manner assist, and might seriously embarrass, the search. The hour of departure was late, and although Masarah urged haste upon the rowers, it was realized that before they could reach the home of the adon, night would have fallen, and, except in the way of preparation, very little could be accomplished before morning. Bariet told Masarah of his vision, and she accepted it as a reality, not caring to speculate upon the question as to how it were possible for the adon to have discovered Peshala in the darkness and secured mastery over him. For the greater part of the journey she remained silent, intent upon some plan by which to secure the release of Martiesen, should it turn out that he was in the hands of Totoes and his followers.

There was less of fear and distress in the villa during the period of darkness than in most parts of Egypt. The few words spoken by Masarah before her departure inspired the hope in Panas that the plague would not be of long duration, and he was thus able to quiet the apprehensions of the adon's noble guests. Serah constantly moved among the women and servants, speaking words of consolation, and assuring her wards that the anger of the Hebrew God was not directed against them, but against the proud and arrogant king. When the light returned, the princes awaited the coming of Martiesen through a portion of the day, but as they were anxious for the safety of their friends, they departed in the afternoon on the journey to Rameses, more than half expecting to find the adon at the capital. The occurrence of the plague disarranged all plans for the proposed uprising, and it was agreed with Panas that until the adon should communicate with them, they would take no further steps. Hence, when Masarah and Bariet reached their destination, the household was assuming something of its accustomed tranquility.

Late in the evening, as the four were discussing plans for the morrow, a servant interrupted them with the announcement that a villager had arrived with an important message, which he wished to deliver to the lieutenant. The man, when admitted, stated that he came from a village at which the barge of the princes had stopped, to allow some of the dancers to disembark. Soon after leaving the village, they had picked up a drifting boat, which bore the cartouche of the adon Martiesen. In the boat was Peshala, the adon's secretary, in whom the spark of life burned so dimly that it could only with difficulty be discerned. The barge returned to the village with the boat in tow, and the present messenger was employed to bring it to the villa, where attention might be given to the dying man. The princes, having heard nothing of the perfidy of Peshala, supposed that he was on his way to Rameses with his master, who they feared must have perished.

Panas and Bariet ran to the landing, and the Libyan was carried to one of the houses lining the approach, where an attempt was made at once to revive him. It was realized that if he could be brought to consciousness, he might be induced to give information concerning the fate of his master. They administered nourishment and restoratives with extreme caution, and in time some slight improvement in his condition was noted. Towards morning he began to mumble words in his own language, and Bariet, who understood the Libyan tongue, sat where he could catch the words, hoping thus to obtain a clue. The man spoke no intelligible sentence, except to rave against the darkness and promise himself requital for the wounds he had received at the hands of Elisheba. Later he spoke Martiesen's name, and then some of the scenes of that terrible night mingled with his babbling in oft-repeated confusion. Only this they learned, that Peshala spoke as though he had Martiesen bound and helpless before him, and was withholding his hand from dealing him a death-blow until he could cause greater anguish of mind through indignities which he intended to inflict.

"This delirium may last several days," said Masarah, who had been listening to the disconnected ravings as they were interpreted by Bariet. "We cannot await his return to consciousness if we would aid Martiesen. We must seek the adon at Manhotef."

"I so believe," assented Panas, "and will at once set about summoning whatever force we have at the villa. The start shall be made at the earliest moment."

"No, Panas, in that way you will not be successful. Should you go with armed men to Manhotef, you would find only the ruins. Those who have lived there have discovered, in their years of wandering among the broken tombs and temples, many places in which they may disappear when danger threatens. Without the aid of more slaves than the Pharaoh himself commands, you would not discover the adon in months."

"Alone, then, or with but one companion, I will go among them in search of my master."

"And become a prisoner with him, thus adding to the amount of ransom that will be demanded."

"But have you not said that we must move quickly if we would aid him? We cannot sit here in idleness and await the turn of events. Martiesen would not do so, were I in need of his aid."

"I will go to Manhotef, and Serah with me," replied Masarah.

Panas leaped to his feet. "Impossible, Masarah! It is most dangerous, and I cannot permit it. Besides, what can two women do among wretches like those who infest the ruins?"

The woman smiled, but made no reply.

"Serah," he said, turning to the girl, "surely you must realize the danger of this. Join me in dissuading your mother from her purpose. Do you think that I, who am able to cope with a score of these rascals, will suffer helpless women to take up the risk that lies in such an enterprise?"

"Nay, Panas, have no fears," said Serah, approaching him and reaching her hand up to his sturdy shoulders. "With my mother, disguised as a worker of magic, I have three times visited Manhotef, and we came thence without inter-ference. I, too, wore disguise, for my face was stained until it was no longer fair, my hair was tossed in tangled mats, and I wore the tattered garments of an insane beggar. Even you would not recognize me when I am thus clad, my Panas."

The lieutenant drew the beautiful girl to his side, and declared again that he would not suffer her to take the risk.

"But there is no risk, Panas," she replied

earnestly. "You should have seen my mother work enchantments before their wondering eyes, and heard how they believed it all; and when she read the horoscope for some, they whispered to one another that she was greater than the oracle at the temple of Apis, who catches the words from the sacred bull itself. They did not know that from one who had escaped them, and had become once more a respectable man, she had learned the history of many in Manhotef, and was thus prepared to tell them truths." And the girl laughed as she recalled the awe in which they held her mother.

"Even old Totoes, who knows something of magic himself, fears my mother," continued Serah, "and when I walked slowly toward him as in a trance, and sang a wild chant, in which he was promised great riches, should he take steps to uncover a vast treasure that had been walled up in one of the houses of the ruin, he thought I possessed the gift of second sight, and, taking my mother aside, promised her half of all he should find, if by her necromancy she would point out where in that mass of ruined palaces and temples he must dig."

"Ah, Serah, one who did not know might think

that you find happiness in deception," said Panas, laughing in spite of himself.

"Nay, Panas," replied Serah, quickly chiding him, "not when deception harms or misleads those who have truth in themselves; but in the case of this old tyrant, who rules the poor wretches at Manhotef by playing upon their superstition, the opportunity was one I could not miss."

"There is no other way of saving the life of the adon, if he be yet alive and at Manhotef," said Masarah, "and before the coming of night we must be upon the way."

"But still I feel that I should be near at hand, ready to render assistance," persisted Panas.

"Such a course would be discovered and endanger our lives, which are otherwise safe," declared Masarah.

Nevertheless, after much persuasion, Panas secured Masarah's assent to this arrangement: He would go with Bariet to a point on the river nearly opposite Manhotef, where they would remain disguised as trappers, engaged in snaring wildfowl. Constant watch would be kept, and by an agreed signal the men might be summoned.

Knowing that at least he would be at no great

distance from the beautiful girl to whom he had
surrendered his heart, the lieutenant consented
to the proposed visit under these conditions.

A trustworthy servant was put in charge of the
babbling but incoherent secretary, and those
upon whom so much depended sought rest. In
the afternoon Serah and Panas met in the magnificent gardens of the villa, and wandered in the
groves, or sat by ponds, talking such nonsense as
lovers in all ages have found pleasure in
discussing. There was much of the airy and joyous
about Serah, which, to the grave soldier, whose
life had mostly been spent in camp and upon
long campaigns in distant countries, appeared
like the butterfly that spreads its gorgeous wings
before each flower; yet he knew that underneath
all this exuberance was hidden the thoughtful,
true woman; for had he not seen how nobly she
could work, and how entirely self-reliant she was
at a time when the strongest hearts turned faint
and sick with fear?

Towards evening Masarah came to them, and
told her daughter it was time to prepare for their
departure.

"Now look well upon me, Panas," said the girl,
"for under the hands of the mother who gave me

all you have been praising these many hours, I am soon to change my form. When next you see me, you will turn away in disgust."

"That cannot be," declared Panas, "for no art, however cunning, can hide the beauty of Serah, nor could I ever behold her other than with pleasure."

"Remember your words, Panas, and expect to regret their utterance," laughed the girl, as she curtsied prettily before him, and turned laughingly away.

An hour later, Panas, clad as a huntsman, with Bariet as his servant, awaited Masarah and Serah in a room adjoining the one occupied by Peshala. When the women finally appeared, the lieutenant rubbed his eyes, and stared as though he beheld an apparition. Masarah was bent, aged in every feature, and showed the black and swarthy complexion of one who lives constantly in the sun. Her clothing befitted her calling, and was hung with oddly-shaped objects and charms. She carried a bronze lamp, or censer, and in a bag at her side were many herbs and bits of wood not common to Egypt. Serah had been darkened with some lotion that gave her a cadaverous, deathlike appearance, and took from her features those delicious curves which were half her charm. Her hair hung in matted tangles about her face and shoulders, and bits of papyrus leaves and stubble clung to it, as though she made her bed in stables. Her eyes had lost their twinkle of fun and love of life, and were now vacant and expressionless, while, by skillful shading about the mouth, her lips were made to look shrunken and ugly. Her arms appeared to be bony, and they carried several unsightly scars; about her feet and ankles cumbersome and frayed strips of cloth were braided. Her clothing was a mass of tatters and patches, so coarse and stained that one would shrink instinctively from it. Indeed, nothing more repulsive or unlovely could be imagined, and it was small wonder that Panas at first thought he was the victim of a deception, and that those before him were women procured for the occasion.

Serah approached him, staring vacantly as though at the wall beyond, and when she reached his side, she awaited his careful inspection. The lieutenant scanned her from head to foot, and was about to turn away, when she bowed gravely, and broke into rippling laughter.

"Would the gallant Panas, who has sworn fifty

times this afternoon that I was the most beautiful woman in Egypt, take back his troth?" she asked naively.

He saw the light and mischief in her eyes, and heard the ring of the voice, and the music of the laughter that had been wont to stir his heart, but otherwise she was a stranger.

"Is it Serah?" and he touched her hand in wonderment, not yet convinced that such complete disguise was possible. At length he said: "I am defeated, for I thought my love would expose the counterfeit, no matter how cunningly it might be made. Had I not heard your voice, and did I not know that your heart is this moment throbbing with the love you but this day pledged me, I should mourn Serah as one who is among the dead."

"And do you doubt that the sorceress and her daughter may with safety visit old Totoes in his ruins?"

"No longer, my loved one. I am only grieved that the hardship should fall upon you. But go, and remember that upon the shore of the Nile opposite Manhotef, I with Bariet shall keep constant watch, and if by night we see a swaying light, or if by day a fluttering piece of cloth thrice raised and lowered, we shall come with all speed to your rescue."

"Fear not, Panas," she replied, "I shall have courage and happiness in the thought that you are near, for you have won my love. The people of Manhotef know us only as you see us now, and they will not suspect our errand."

The women walked rapidly to the landing-place, where a small boat was ready for them. Serah took the oars, and with a wave of her hand to the anxious lieutenant, they started directly across the river. Panas gave orders that the most careful watch should be kept upon the Libyan at all hours, and a few minutes after the departure of Masarah and Serah, he entered the boat with Bariet, and made all speed toward the rendezvous agreed upon.

∩|||||

CHAPTER XV

AT MANHOTEF

MANY hours after Martiesen had been carried away from the lagoon, he opened his eyes to consciousness. About him all was intensely dark, and his first thought was that he was still upon the Nile with Peshala; but when his hands were extended, they came against the damp and trodden surface of an earthen floor. It required time for him to collect his thoughts — to determine where he was when he lost himself, or what had taken place just before that moment. He had a dim recollection of sudden passion, and then a leap and a grasp upon a man's throat. Who was this he sought to kill? Ah, yes, Peshala! He recalled it now — the man was Peshala. But what had passed before? Was there cause why he should seek the life of Peshala? He asked this question many times before the light at last broke through, and he remembered that he was searching for Elisheba, and that Peshala had guided him to Manhotef, and that Elisheba was not there. But where was Peshala now? Had he escaped? Or had his life gone out as Martiesen intended it should, and was not the body near him on the floor? Martiesen felt on each side as far as he could reach, and found upon his left and at his head a stone wall, upon the other side, only the beaten earth. He could not rise, for his brain whirled, and he grew deathly faint when he attempted it. There was a bandage about his head, and under it some leaves, the bruised pulp of which crumpled in his fingers. Who had wrapped his head in this poultice? Surely not Peshala, for the secretary, if he had escaped, would not have bound the wounds of one whose life he sought.

Thus, half-conscious, and with throbbing, fainting head, the adon's thoughts ran in a circle, and ever returned to the one reality — that he was wounded, helpless, and alone. After a time, he spoke, feebly at first, but later with more volume. He called for water, repeating the word many times with all his strength, until in time he saw the glimmer of a lamp approaching through a long and narrow passageway. Then a man came to his side, and held the lamp where its dim light fell on the adon's face.

"Water, water!" pleaded Martiesen. "I thirst greatly."

The man, a convict, shorn of both ears, raised a small jar from the floor, and with the swinging lamp went slowly back the way he came. The adon may have swooned, for he did not realize the convict's return, until he felt a hand under his head, and the edge of the water jar at his lips. He drank deeply, a bitter, medicated draught, but he cared not if it were poisoned, so long as it quenched his thirst. When he had drained the vessel, he sank upon his pillow of rags, and murmured a prayer to Osiris for those who succored him.

And when he looked again, two men were beside him, the priest Totoes and the convict Niston, crouching near with the lamp between them.

"What place is this?" asked the adon, when he had rested.

"Manhotef, my lord adon," answered Totoes, quietly.

"Into whose hands have I fallen?" he questioned, after a wait of some minutes.

"The hands of friends, who found you unconscious and wounded on the bank of the Nile," declared Totoes.

"Wounded? and by whom?"

"By the man with whom you fought in the boat, and who suddenly overcame you. Then, after dealing you a blow with one of the oars, he threw you into the shallow water, and rowed rapidly away. Niston, who saw the encounter, took you from the river in time to preserve your life." The convict grinned, and nodded assent.

"Why am I imprisoned?"

"Not imprisoned, my lord adon," responded Totoes, quickly. "You are not imprisoned, but concealed in a place where you will not be discovered by enemies, for you are not in condition to meet them. My lord adon needs rest, and he must talk no more at present."

Martiesen felt a delicious numbness stealing over him, and it came to his mind that the water of which he drank so freely was drugged. He made an effort to shake off his drowsiness.

"Stay, priest! Were any strangers found within your harbor when the darkness broke?" he demanded.

"When my lord adon is further refreshed, I shall talk with him," said Totoes. "Niston will remain within call." And through his closing eyelids Martiesen saw the men depart, with the smoking lamp between them.

When he next awoke, the adon's first thought was that he was greatly strengthened, yet every muscle was cramped and lame from lying for hours upon the hard ground. He shouted for the convict, and after the call was several times repeated, Niston came sleepily along the passageway, as one but that moment aroused from his couch.

"Is it day or night?" the adon asked.

"Night," was the answer. "But you are not to talk until Totoes comes."

"Totoes?"

"Aye, the priest who was with you here when first you awoke."

"What has this priest to do with me, and why has he brought me to an underground tomb, for such I see it is?" demanded Martiesen.

"My lord, I am to answer no questions, for Totoes, whom I have summoned, will tell you all. I have orders to give you food and drink and to care for your wound, but no more."

Niston returned to the outer room, and soon brought some lentils, cakes, and goat's milk, of which the adon partook with relish. In the meantime the convict prepared a fresh poultice of cooling leaves, which he bound upon the adon's head with a dexterity that spoke of long practice. The adon noticed that the convict watched him narrowly, and at all times kept near the passageway, as if anticipating an attempted escape.

"You guard me closely," he said.

"I do as I am told, Martiesen, and those who know the master of Manhotef learn to do his bidding."

"When am I to see my captor again, this master of Manhotef, as you call him?"

"He gave orders to be informed at once, should you awake, and he is now upon his way hither."

Taking up the basket and jar in which the food and water were brought, the convict, keeping his face toward the adon, walked backward through the passageway. Martiesen watched him closely, and observed that the barrier separating the outer chamber from the passageway was opened from the outside, doubtless by one on guard at that point. In a few moments the stone turned upon its grooves again, and Totoes came forward.

"My lord adon improves rapidly," he said, seating himself just inside the chamber.

"Aye, I am stronger now, and must thank you, and those who serve you, for both food and attention. I hope you will not find me ungrateful, sir priest. I assure you that you shall be well rewarded. At this moment, however, I am most impatient for an answer to a question I asked before I fell into the stupor brought upon me by your potion. I think you remember it: Were any strangers discovered in your harbor when the darkness left?"

"Yes, my lord adon, I recall your question, and will answer. There were in the harbor two beautiful Hebrew girls, sisters I believe, and they were held by two slaves, their captors."

Martiesen started from the ground. "Where are they, priest? Quick, where are they?"

"Slowly, slowly, my lord," replied Totoes, craftily. "Do not overexcite yourself, and you shall hear all. My people, stirred by the accursed plague, were early abroad when light appeared, and some of them saw within the harbor a barge upon which were the sisters. Two slaves guarded them, and it was evident that the maidens were in great fear and distress. A messenger hastily brought me the tidings, and on running to the shore I found the report true. Determined to assist the women, I directed several men to surround the barge, but when I demanded surrender, the slaves resisted so vigorously that, before we overpowered and slew them, three of my followers fell at their hands."

"But the sisters? Tell me quickly, priest, where are they? I care not for this story of a fight between slaves and your wretched followers. Where are the Hebrew women?"

"They are here, at Manhotef."

"Here!"

The priest nodded.

"Safe and unharmed?"

"They are safe and unharmed, for which they have to thank my bravery and that of my followers, three of whom, as I tell you, gave up their lives. I myself received a blow that nearly blinded me, as you can see."

"Enough, Totoes, for such the convict tells me is your name. Let the description of the fight remain for the future. I would see the Hebrew sisters at once."

"Nay, my lord adon, again you are in too great haste. The ruins of Manhotef are wide, and its roads are difficult to follow, even to those who are strong. Then there is another reason for patience. Peshala, your secretary, was the one with whom you fought in the boat, and when he left you for dead in the shallow water near the mouth of the harbor, he took the way to Rameses. On the day preceding a certain festival given for the princes of the blood at the home of Martiesen, Peshala sent me a writing, in which he disclosed the existence of a plot to usurp the throne, of which my lord may have heard."

The adon gave no answer.

"Peshala informed me that he should go to Rameses that night, to expose the conspiracy to the Pharaoh. On a previous occasion he had sought me, and endeavored to secure my aid in carrying out plans formed by him for your confusion; but I did not enter into them, as I have ever entertained great respect for the wise and gentle ruler of the Nome of the Prince. However, I owe something to Peshala for his aid in certain enterprises, and so, when he asked a promise of me to the effect that if he would leave two Hebrew girls in the harbor, I would conduct them to a safe hiding-place and guard them until his return, I gave it freely."

"And you intend to do this?"

"My lord adon, I am an outcast priest, driven from home and temple by cunning and unscrupulous enemies, who, fortunately for them, secured the favor of the ruler. In Manhotef there are very many wretches that look to me for direction and advice. If I fail them, they must starve in these ruined tombs and temples, which produce only bats. We are an impoverished people."

"And has Peshala promised you treasure?"

"The promise has been made."

"Then you ask ransom before you will set the Hebrew sisters and myself free?"

"It is so, my lord. We at Manhotef must surely cast our seed when the waters rise."

"What sum do you demand?"

"Ten thousand talents in gems and bars of gold and silver."

"The sum is large."

"The service is greater."

"You surely cannot expect as much from Peshala, who has nothing."

"With the Pharaoh as his benefactor, he has everything, even that which Martiesen calls his own."

The adon hesitated. From the first he had entertained doubts as to the truth of the priest's tale, and at this moment a cunning gleam, which the flickering lamp disclosed in the eyes of his jailer, deepened his belief that most of what he had heard was false.

"How do you propose this sum shall be paid?"

"The adon is a scholar. With his own hand let him write an order to his lieutenant Panas, and set his cartouche at the bottom. It shall direct the payment of the treasure to the bearer, and give him safe passage from the adon's palace."

"And what guarantee have I that when the sum is paid we shall be set free?"

"The pledge of Totoes, which in Manhotef is as good as law, as is the command of Meneptah in Rameses."

Martiesen looked into his face, and smiled.

"You doubt, my lord?"

"Aye, Totoes, I doubt. I would not withhold this treasure nor twice its volume, if it were in your power to free Elisheba and Abigail, the Hebrew sisters, and with myself set us upon the Nile in a craft that will bear us hence. Nay, you may accompany us, and with you the earless convict, or any of your thieves, and I will pledge the honor of a house that has never been sullied to pay the treasure to your hands and offer no resistance to your return. But without any assurance that you hold Elisheba captive, or that she is living, and has her sister with her, or that you will even free me from this tomb, once you get my order for the ransom, except only the promise you offer, I will not give you treasure."

"As my lord adon wishes," said the priest, rising. "Two days have passed since you were brought here. You know full well that Peshala will not be slow to act. I cannot tell at what hour he may come with forces at his command and the authority of the Egyptian king as his warrant. I have no choice whether the treasure is paid at your hands or at the hands of Peshala, but this I know, you will not see the light of day or any face but mine, nor will I release the woman who is so greatly coveted by both the adon and his secretary, until I hold the treasure I have named secure in Manhotef."

Taking the lamp in his hand, Totoes strode down the passageway, and Martiesen heard the stone which closed the entrance roll into place. The adon knew there was no hope of escape, for just beyond this massive stone was a room similar to the one in which he was confined. When he crept through the passageway, he heard the voices of Totoes and Niston, and though he could distinguish no words, he knew they sat on guard.

Six hours passed before the priest appeared

again, though to the lonely occupant of this chamber the hours might have been days, so slowly did they drag. A small quantity of food and water was brought, and the adon was told to eat and drink. Totoes asked no questions, until he took up the lamp to depart, and then he inquired if the adon was yet willing to execute the writing directing Panas to pay the ransom.

"Nay, priest," he replied, "it is idle to ask, for I have no surety that those for whom you demand ransom will be released. Your conditions do not inspire confidence, and I have no faith in your pledge."

"When Peshala stands here beside me with an order from the Pharaoh in his hands for your arrest, the hour will have passed in which you may accept this offer."

There was no reply, and Totoes again left the chamber to its despairing occupant. How long a time elapsed before the next visit, Martiesen could not tell. He spent hours in pacing the walled room; then, though he was familiar with the character of such enclosures, and knew the uselessness of his search, he spent other hours in passing his hands over every inch of the wall, hoping he might find one stone that could be loosened, and open an opportunity to dig toward freedom. He searched the passage to the outer chamber, listened long at the stone door, and tried his strength upon its grooves. He slept, and at last, upon waking, found Totoes by his side. The priest, as before, had brought food and drink.

"I have pleasant tidings for you, my lord adon," said Totoes, as Martiesen ate ravenously of the scanty fare.

"Indeed, that is good of you," answered Martiesen, as he glowered upon the priest, and saw his face was overspread with a grin.

"Yes, tidings from Rameses, where your secretary has been added to the list of counselors and favorites of the Pharaoh."

"Excellent. Then I suppose Totoes anticipates an early return to his caste and his temple, with ten thousand talents in his bag. But who brings these tidings thither?"

"Last night there came to Manhotef from Rameses a soothsayer and practicer of magic, accompanied by her insane daughter. She is a shrewd and cunning hag, who has been here before, and, though I have endeavored to discover the secret of her tricks, I have failed. She travels up and down the Nile, and often displays her art in the homes of the rich. I am told that she is much sought by those who have love affairs in which they wish advice."

"Her name — perhaps I know her!"

"Masarah — — — "

The basin which Martiesen was raising to his lips dropped from his hands, and the water was spilled upon the floor. But the adon quickly recovered himself from the surprise occasioned by the name Totoes had spoken.

"Your pardon, priest," he said with apparent regret over the accident. "In my greediness to quench my thirst the basin slipped, and I remain thirsty. I suppose it would be a breach of the rules of your prison to ask for a renewal of the water. The name, you say, is —— "

"Masarah."

"No, I know it not. There are so many women of her class. But this one, you say, has a daughter."

"Aye, insane and strange, but sometimes cunning with her songs and mysteries, in which she helps her mother; an ugly-looking creature, though she has a voice of strange power and sweetness."

"The mother?"

"Nay, the daughter. The mother is a crone."

"I do not recognize your description, and if I

have ever seen them, have forgotten it. But what says this Ma——, Ma—— "

"Masarah," prompted the priest.

"What says this Masarah about the Pharaoh and his new-found confidant? Come, Totoes, speak, and it may win the order for my ransom."

"My lord adon, you mistake me," replied Totoes, in a spirit of protest. "I desire to set you and these maidens free, for I have little love for the king or for Peshala. The rich and powerful so often forget the poor and helpless, when a service has been rendered, and there is no longer need for aid, that in justice to those for whom I act here in Manhotef, I have demanded the ransom treasure in advance of your freedom."

"Big fish are not often caught in your net, Totoes, and so you intend to bring this one to a landing," laughed the adon.

"You do not look at it from an entirely false position, my lord," admitted the priest.

"But tell me of Rameses, Totoes; we shall speak of the ransom later."

"Masarah and her daughter were in Rameses during the plague of darkness, which, she says, was sent at the instance of Moses, the prophet of the Hebrews. Yesterday they went to the palace with others of their kind, to show their arts before the king, his nobles, and his women. While there, they heard talk concerning a new-found favorite who had done the king some great service, and when Masarah made inquiry, she learned that his name was Peshala. She was told that Peshala had exposed a plot to usurp the crown in which you were to some extent concerned, and there was talk that your estates are to be sequestered to the crown, and a generous reward conferred upon your former scribe. All this I drew from her by many questions," declared the priest.

"Likelier she drew it from you," thought Martiesen, but aloud he said: "The tidings are grave, if true, and I do not like the story, for it has an ugly look. Do you believe the woman, Totoes?"

"I do, my lord. Upon such matters women of this class tell their gossip faithfully. Were it a court scandal, involving the character of some other woman, there might be cause to doubt."

"May I not see her and question her myself?" asked Martiesen.

The priest looked at his prisoner searchingly. He felt that the ransom was now almost within his grasp, and if he would win it, he must partially allay the adon's suspicions. A denial of the request might further arouse them, and this Totoes could not afford to do. He resolved to employ a semblance of frankness, hoping thus to disarm the man he was attempting to rob. Moreover, he believed that through the giving of promises he could induce Masarah to add such details to the story as might be necessary to carry out the deception.

"My lord, they may have departed," replied Totoes, "but I will seek them, and if Masarah will return, you may question her in my presence, in the outer chamber of the tomb."

Totoes hurried away, and when the stone was rolled to its place, Martiesen leaped to his feet, and ran from side to side of the circumscribed place in excess of joy. Hope came again to his heart, for he read in the presence of Masarah an attempt to effect the escape of Elisheba and Abigail, if they were prisoners, and possibly of himself.

CHAPTER XVI

EASY MAGIC

THE tomb in which Martiesen was confined was one of a score of the same general character and appearance which found their entrances in the once splendid court of the dismantled temple. It was reached by a long, descending passage, narrow, low, and walled. The first or outer chamber was for the accommodation of relatives of the deceased, who at stated intervals brought hither food and offerings for the dead. Then another passage led to the middle chamber, and in this the mummified bodies were placed. Immediately adjoining this, and separated by a strong wall, was a smaller chamber, which the souls of the dead were supposed to occupy. Blocking the passage between the outer and middle chambers was a heavy mass of granite, balanced with such precision that it would move back easily from the outside, but could not be lifted from its bed by anyone stationed in the passage leading to the interior rooms.

Totoes therefore felt secure in leaving the convicts Niston and Tarta on guard in the outer chamber, and after repeated cautioning and the promise of a speedy return, he crept through the inclined passage, and sought Masarah in the ruin-piled streets of Manhotef. The evening was falling when he came to an open space in which a number of raggedly-clad men, women and children were seated in a semicircle, watching the preparations going on before them. Around the little space, heaped in strange confusion, were hundreds of splendid blocks of carved marble, and upon these lounged the men, scarcely less interested in what they saw than were the awestricken women and the fearsome children huddled together upon the ground.

A few yards of cloth thrown over some bamboo rods served as a screen, and in front of this was a small heap of flickering embers. As the darkness deepened, Masarah, slowly chanting a shrill refrain, approached the glowing coals, and, as she muttered incantations that were scarcely heard beyond the reach of her staff, she sprinkled a powdered substance upon the fire. A white smoke arose, and as the witch-like woman waved her arms, grotesque shapes of giant size formed from the smoke, and danced their way into the evening sky. They were merry, pleasing ghosts, and as they danced and bowed before each other, Serah brought colored lights from behind the screen, and by waving them aloft lighted the apparitions with brilliant hues.

There were expressions of delight from those who beheld the apparitions, and into the wan faces of the children came some glimmer of happiness. The women, too, lost for a moment the starved, hunted look which they ever bore at Manhotef, and one of them beckoned furtively to the soothsayer to approach. When Masarah stood by her side, still waving her wand, the woman spoke, without turning her eyes from the figures.

"Osiris reward you," said the woman. "You have brought back the memory of the happy days I lived in Rameses."

"Why did you come here?" asked Masarah, as though mumbling her incantations.

"My husband fell a victim to Totoes, and engaged with him in a plot. We fled thither to escape the mines."

"Where is your husband now?"

"Alas! He planned to escape and seek asylum in Nubia, and was killed by the guards."

"Are you guilty of crime?"

"As Aupee is my watchful friend, I am not. But Totoes has ordered that I come to his castle to serve as his slave, and this is my last night of happiness. Osiris defend me from the fate."

Masarah dropped her wand, and as she stooped to pick it up, glanced at the woman. She was young and pretty, not much older than her own daughter, and with a depth of anguish in her wonderful eyes that touched the heart of the sorceress with sympathy.

"I read in the stars that help is at hand," said Masarah, while Serah sprinkled more powder upon the coals, and fresh smoke arose. "Tell me this, has Totoes a noble prisoner here in Manhotef?"

"Yes, two men were speaking about it as they gambled here while you were erecting your screen."

"Where confined?"

"In one of the tombs underneath the ruins of the great temple. The men said that heavy ransom would be demanded."

"Will gold help you to escape?"

"Gold! O mighty Nub! Ah, my father has gold, and is a merchant in Rameses; but he knows not where I am. Gold! With gold, or even silver, I could bribe my way hence. No one in Manhotef has gold, except the terrible ruler."

Masarah swept her tattered robe around her, until it almost covered her face, and as she moved forward, she stumbled against the woman with whom she had spoken. A small purse filled with tiny gold rings fell into the woman's lap, but she covered it with her hand so quickly that none saw, especially as they were watching the magic-worker.

Masarah presented a number of simple tricks of magic, and was about to close her performance with the usual appeal for gifts of food or small coins, when she saw the tall form of the deposed priest approaching from a distance. As he came near, Totoes paused a few moments, and watched the exhibition. Then he came into the circle, where he could catch the eye of Masarah, and signified that he sought her. The woman soon ceased her magic, and stepped to one side, where she could converse privately with the priest.

Serah took up a weird chant, which caused a nervous craning of necks over the shoulders of her hearers, and while this was going on, she prepared to pack their meager paraphernalia in the baskets in which it was carried. The people hastened away as if fearful of the master who had interrupted their poor pleasure.

"Would it not better please Masarah to earn a large sum of gold by one bold stroke than to spend her life amusing beggars for mean bits of base metal?" the priest asked her abruptly.

She looked at him inquiringly. "What means the priest of Manhotef by such a question? Does he not know that the struggle of the poor is ever for gold — gold — ever for gold? Aye, and that even the rich, who have it in abundance, never tire, never rest from its pursuit?"

"Your trade is one of deception in small matters, which, I grant, do little harm, as they serve simply to amuse by mild fright. What if the deceptions were exercised in a larger field, where they still would do no harm, except to alarm? Would the magic-worker hesitate?"

"The priest of Manhotef speaks in riddles. We who have intercourse with the gods and strange spirits may do nothing to anger the dead; nor, if we would work without molestation, may we do that of which our rulers do not approve."

"Even so. But this of which I speak would displease neither the gods, the dead, nor the rulers."

"Then it can contain no harm, for if we displease not the gods, we wrong not the living; if we bring no dishonor upon the dead, we cherish their memory; if we obey our rulers, we complete our full duty."

"Masarah is wise, and I see that she may be trusted. When I have disclosed my plan, she can decide whether it will conflict with her practice. There is concealed in one of the temple tombs a nobleman who is greatly interested in affairs at Rameses. While upon a visit to him some hours ago, I told him that a magic-worker and her daughter were in Manhotef, and that they lately came from the court; and thinking to beguile his time, and further prepare his mind to accept certain propositions I have made him, I gave him tidings from Rameses, which he supposes were brought thence by you. He became so deeply interested that he requested further details from your own lips. It is a harmless story, but if you will consent to carry out the deception, he can be brought to put into my hands treasure that will enrich us both."

The woman did not reply immediately, and appeared to be thinking. Finally she answered: "I like not the looks of it, Totoes. I fear no good will come of it. Is this nobleman your prisoner?"

"Nay, he is but seeking asylum from impending danger."

"You put it cleverly, sir priest, but Masarah reads what you would conceal. You wish to extort ransom."

Totoes laughed. "Ah, Masarah, were those who rule Egypt as wise as the soothsayer, our troubles would be lessened. You read aright! I ask ransom for his release, and if he may be made to think that the danger is pressing, he will pay it."

Though Totoes had not spoken the adon's name, Masarah was certain that Martiesen was the prisoner to whom he referred, and so in time she consented to join the deception. Thereupon Totoes put her in possession of the whole story, and coached her in what he wished her to say. Masarah gave him grave attention, though underneath the impassive exterior displayed to the priest she was palpitating with excitement.

"Now you know the tale as I would have him

hear it," said Totoes, "and you are cunning enough not to be caught with his questions."

"Never fear, Totoes," she replied with a marked twinkle in her eyes, "for I will tell him many strange things, if they but advance your interests, and you pay me well for the service."

"Indeed, that I will, if you picture the scene at Rameses with a vivid dash of probability."

"There is no harm in this," she replied. "He doubtless has more wealth than his requirements."

"Aye, that he has; and, what is more, he has not been generous with it to the poor."

"But I cannot go into the tombs from which the bodies have been taken, and in which the souls yet remain, unless I first exercise certain spells and arts by which the spirits of those who may be disturbed shall be propitiated."

"I have no objection to that," said Totoes, "for while your magic will not harm the dead, it will serve to amuse the living. I ask only that you tell my guest the story of the new favorite of the king at Rameses, and tell it well. Come, strike your tent, and we shall go at once."

"Not now," replied Masarah. "I and my daughter are wearied and need rest, for the day in Manhotef has been long, and the labor tiresome and of little profit. When this star reaches here," she said, pointing to the zenith, "we shall be before the temple."

"That will be midnight," said the priest.

"What matters that to Totoes, who keeps his guest underground?" asked the woman, quickly.

"Nothing, nor does it matter to the guest," replied the priest with a laugh, as he moved away.

"But it matters to Masarah," said the sorceress under her breath, "for at that hour the poor wretches in Manhotef will sleep."

CHAPTER XVII

NECROMANCY

THE approach of Totoes through the passage to the chamber in which Martiesen was imprisoned, was a signal to the adon that the time for him to act had come. He was confident that Masarah would form some plan to aid him in escaping, and he decided to await its development before taking the initiative himself. Martiesen's heart leaped with hope when Totoes informed him that the sorceress was in the outer chamber, and would answer all questions after she had performed her charms, for he looked upon this as more than halfway on the road to freedom. Once beyond that stone at the end of the passageway, and he would never return to this room again. He was unarmed, but believed that by quick surprise he could break through the guard, and gain his liberty. If not, he could die in a bold attempt.

The priest produced a mask, which he advised the adon to wear, so that the woman would not know to whom she spoke. Without demur, Martiesen consented to its adjustment, and he followed his captor to the outer room. Martiesen noted that Niston and Tarta guarded the opposite entrance, and were well supplied with weapons, with which to resist an attempt to escape. Apparently the sorceress and her daughter did not observe his arrival. He marveled at their disguise, and with difficulty brought himself to believe they were not impostors, who had stolen the name of the famous soothsayer and her daughter.

In the center of the room stood a large brazier, and ranged upon the earthen floor beside it were several small vessels. Grouped against the wall were the baskets and paraphernalia which the women carried. When the priest and Martiesen were seated, Masarah applied fire to the substance within the brazier, and, kneeling with her daughter beside the vessel, they began a low, monotonous chant, in which they implored the souls of those for whom this tomb had been built to rest content, for they had come hither to do no violence. The odor of pleasant spices filled the place, and an agreeable light shone upon the walls, and softened their dark and rugged surfaces. The low crooning of the women was not unmusical, and a delicious drowsiness came to the senses of the watching men.

"She is mistress of the art," whispered Totoes, in admiration. "Watch her well, my lord adon, and you will see many wonders."

When the incantation was concluded, Masarah arose, and taking a vessel from the ground, asked that it be filled with water. From a large jar near the entrance, Niston brought the required liquid. She turned a portion into a small cup, or basin, and carried it to her mouth.

"You do well, sir priest," she said, after she had tasted the contents, "to serve wine so freely."

"If you call that wine," said Totoes, laughing, "you are easily satisfied, for the Nile is a goodly stream."

"Nay, but you jest," replied Masarah. "This which I poured from the vessel that Niston brought is wine, as your guest will tell you."

She approached and handed the basin to Martiesen, who, moving his mask slightly aside, tasted, and pronounced the liquor as good wine as he had ever drunk.

"Then drink your fill," said Masarah. And the adon drained the bowl.

"Will Totoes pledge his guest in wine of his own providing?" asked the sorceress.

"Nay, of your providing," contended the priest. "The jar contains water from the Nile, and it was brought here by Niston and Tarta last night at no little trouble. If Masarah can make wine of it, then she would better give up other sorceries, and tell the Hebrew prophets that she knows a better trick than turning rivers into blood."

"She surely gave me wine," declared Martiesen, "and I can feel its strength and warmth in my veins."

"Here, convicts, we will convince our host," said Masarah. "Turn this away, and bring again from the jar."

The wondering Niston did as he was bidden, and Masarah again filled the basin from the vessel. This time she handed it to Totoes, and insisted that he satisfy himself.

The priest sipped the liquid, and peered into the basin. He drew the aroma to his nostrils, then tasted deep, and held it in his mouth as though to test the quality.

"Yes, it is wine," he said. "Surely, woman, you

have learned your magic from the gods, for, as I live, you give me here, from a vessel which a moment ago contained water, as good wine as was ever provided for the table of a priest."

He raised the basin, and drank all it contained.

While Masarah served Niston and Tarta freely from the same vessel, Totoes turned to Martiesen and remarked upon the exceeding cleverness of the trick. "For certainly she does not possess the power of changing Nile water into the juice of grape or the essence of barley. I told you that she was the most wonderful of her caste."

"Nevertheless, I wish she would hasten the exhibition, for I await her story concerning affairs at Rameses with impatience," replied the adon.

Masarah threw a handful of dried leaves upon the brazier, and when they burst into flame, a hue of pale green filled the cell, imparting to each interested spectator a deathlike appearance. Niston, watching intently, swayed a moment, and then fell forward upon his face as though dead. Totoes started up, and attempted to step toward the prostrate convict, but he sank upon his knees, and as a tremor of weakness ran through his body, he braced his hands upon the floor to keep from falling.

"Poisoned!" he cried hoarsely. "You she-fiend of Anpu! You have placed poison in the drink!"

He endeavored to reach the sorceress, bending at arm's length before him over the brazier, but he fell upon the floor, and sank into insensibility.

Tarta started to crawl out of the passageway where he had seen his companion fall, but he had not gone more than twice the length of his body when his arms and limbs failed him, and he fell in deathlike stupor.

"Masarah!" cried the adon, leaping to her side, "was there no other way?"

"They are not dead," she replied with a laugh, "but they will not know it for a full day."

After an examination of the men, the adon was satisfied that they had been given some powerful narcotic, for they were breathing quite as regularly as though in natural slumber.

"Though they were my enemies, and held me prisoner," he said, "I could not rest in peace with the thought that to secure my liberty they were given a fatal draught. I pray you will pardon my suspicion, Masarah, for it was most unjust. However, the scene was so real, so full of terror, and the men were so quickly overcome, that for the moment my only thought was that they had partaken of an active poison, which struck them dead."

"There is no need for apology," said Masarah, "so long as your way to liberty has been opened without murder, if we but hasten to seize the advantage."

"Elisheba and Abigail, where are they?"

"Safe in Zoan."

"In Zoan! Totoes told me they were confined in Manhotef, and he sought to extort ransom for their freedom."

"Aye, no doubt. Totoes is so accustomed to falsehood that he often employs it when the truth would serve his purpose better."

Taking one of the lamps from its hanging, Masarah directed the adon and Serah to drag the unconscious men into the inner passageway, and when this was done, the door was closed upon them, and the lock-stone dropped into place. Masarah was constantly urging haste, and started to lead the way to the entrance, when the adon caught the glitter of gems from a niche in the wall where it was the custom to leave food for the dead. He thrust his hand into the place and drew out the scabbard which had been taken from him by the priest. Upon the floor where Niston fell, he found a knife. Provided with a weapon which he could at least use in defense, he yielded to the woman's urgency, and hurried through the narrow tunnel.

They emerged into a court filled with broken columns and all the debris of a splendid temple of worship, thrown by the grinding wheels of ten centuries into a mass of distressing confusion. The black mouths of a score of similar entrances yawned silently around them. Mighty blocks of granite, poised upon each other at all angles, appeared to shut off every path. Great piles of brick and mortar were scattered amongst the stones, thus increasing the confusion and making it almost impossible in the dim light afforded by the stars to discover a way by which one might escape, and avoid the labor and delay of clambering from one block of marble to another the entire length of the once magnificent structure. Serah touched the adon's arm, and motioned to a low archway under a slab of black marble, which centuries before had been one of the alternate squares of black and white that lined the inner wall. He bent upon his hands and knees, and without question crawled into the narrow exit.

The way was difficult to follow, for it led under considerable sections of the debris, winding close to column bases that sustained the larger blocks and slabs, and thus formed a rough but certain passageway.

At last they stood upright, free from the threatening piles of stone, and brick, and mortar under which they had slowly made their progress. They hastened through the dismantled pylon, and came to the approach. As they moved forward, the savage snarl of a hound came from the shadow of a prostrate dromo, and then, with one loud bay, the animal leaped upon Serah, who was in the lead. Martiesen sprang at the same instant, and catching the dog by the throat before it could fasten its teeth into the crouching girl, he bore the beast down upon the ground, and struck a blow with his knife that found a vital point.

But the bay to which the hound gave tongue as he leaped was taken up by others of his kind, and, to the deep alarm of the adon and his rescuers, they heard the disturbance spreading in every direction. Catching hold of hands, they ran with all possible speed through the ruined streets. Masarah led the way now, and she soon turned from the customary path to the river, and they shortly entered a half-filled ditch, or ancient canal. Walking for a considerable distance in water that came to their knees, they sought the opposite bank, and hurried forward through dense reeds and papyrus. The barking of dogs and shouts of men could be heard behind them, and when they turned back a moment in their flight, they saw the glimmer of rapidly-moving torches. All this furnished reason for greater speed, and so they ran as best they might, until they came upon the mouth of the old ditch, and with great relief entered the boat which Masarah and Serah had concealed in the papyrus upon their arrival at Manhotef. It required but a few moments for Martiesen to row a sufficient distance from the shore to insure their safety, and when this was accomplished, he rested upon his oars, to recover from his exertions.

It was a capital crime to kill a dog in Egypt, and if the adon's advanced intelligence had not to a considerable degree freed him from the superstitions of his people, he might have hesitated, even in that moment of imminent danger, before he struck the blow that ended the life of the priest's hound. But the animal was slain, and when those who were brought from hovels, alarmed by the chorus of barking dogs, were led to the temple approach by these same keen-scented animals sniffing the fresh blood, and there saw the work of some impious hand, they were seized with consternation and anger. They called loudly for Totoes, and a party ran shouting through the ruined city, searching for their leader to avenge the sacrilege. But Totoes could not be found; none had seen him since the evening before, when he conversed aside with the sorceress. Nor were his servants, Niston and Tarta, discovered, and so they surmised that the sorceress had not only made away with the men, as she did with the figures that arose from the fire at her bidding, but had also killed the faithful dog that kept the priest company.

It was known to several that the adon was imprisoned in one of the tombs, for they had assisted in dragging him through the entrance winding under the debris, but so great was the fear of the sorceress that none would venture into the ruin before the coming of day. The dogs soon led a party of the most active searchers to the old canal, and then along its course. Resting quietly in their boat, Masarah, Serah, and Mar-tiesen saw the shadowy forms upon the river's bank, and heard the frightened searchers shout the name of Totoes.

"Aye, that is right," laughed Masarah. "Fill your throats with the name of the cunning leader. Shout all together, and you cannot awaken him before another night."

In a few words Serah possessed Martiesen with the details concerning the escape of Elisheba and Abigail, and the subsequent discovery of Peshala in the drifting boat. The adon directed his boat toward where they might expect Panas and Bariet, but before reaching the center of the river, they were hailed, and in a moment joined by their friends. Bariet, who kept the last watch of the night, had seen the torches upon the shores at Manhotef. He dragged Panas into the boat before the lieutenant was fully awake, and they were hastening to render the assistance which they supposed would be necessary.

After greetings were over, and the boats were turned toward the villa, the adon spoke to Bariet: "I have heard briefly of the service you have rendered those whom I love, and in so doing you have atoned for your crime in aiding Peshala. You are free, Bariet, and if you remain in my service, your station shall be next below that of my faithful Panas."

The Assyrian took the adon's hand, and carried it to his lips. "My debt is not paid, my lord adon. I ask that I may still remain your slave."

Day had fully come when they reached the villa. As they neared the landing, an unusual commotion was observed upon the shore, and a number of servants assembled to meet them. When Martiesen and Panas ascended the steps, the servants to whom had been entrusted the care of Peshala came to them, and announced that the Libyan had escaped.

"Escaped!" cried Panas. "Did I not charge you that constant and most careful watch should be kept upon him?"

"Yea, my lord, it is as Panas says," confessed the man, turning to Martiesen. "Constant watch was kept, but as Peshala apparently continued in stupor, only one attendant was left with him. At daybreak this morning the servant whose duty it was to remain the last half of the night was found dead in the bed, but of Peshala, who occupied the bed before him, there is no trace."

⌒||||||||

CHAPTER XVIII

IN GOSHEN

THE season of the ingathering was at its height. Over all Egypt, with the first appearance of the sun, men and women were daily toiling in the fields, nor did they cease their labors until evening had fallen. In a few weeks swift couriers, trained to great endurance, would dash from post to post, two thousand miles, in light boats, carrying the welcome news that the Nile had commenced to rise, and the Season of the Waters was coming once more, to fill the canals and reservoirs and spread in life-giving flood over the dry and thirsty fields.

From lip to lip the cry would be repeated: "Father Nile is awakening! He comes again in his might to refresh his children! We must hasten with the harvest, my brother, lest he sees that we were careless with what he has given us."

From heart to heart the response would come: "The gods are good indeed! Many days have they journeyed underground, to awaken the sleeping fountains and implore them to pour out their generous wealth, that we may not perish. Yea, my brother, the gods are good indeed."

And then, for fifty-one days following the first increase in the water, the Nile would continue to rise, inch by inch, creeping slowly above its banks, and reaching out over the land like a shallow lake, until it came to full flood. Here it lies, resting after its mighty effort; and then day by day it recedes, yet lingers fondly, as though loath to leave a lover who holds it in such close embrace. One hundred and thirty-one days will pass from that upon which the swelling waters first reach up their heads, before the Nile is once more confined within its channel.

Thousands of years, through the reigns of rulers and dynasties yet unknown, have the people of Egypt ever looked forward with feelings of the greatest happiness to the coming of the inundation, the Season of the Waters. To them no other event of the year was of such importance.

But in this time of harvest they were filled with a nameless dread. So wonderful, so terrible had been the phenomena wrought in their land since the coming of the season of vegetation, each visitation more distressing than the one which passed before, that a fear crept into the hearts of the people, and from this arose a belief that the severest punishment was yet to come. And what more natural than for them to think that this strange new God of the Hebrews would withhold from them the refreshing waters of their beloved river?

So with nervous haste and increasing anxiety they toiled in the harvest fields, hoping for, yet dreading, the arrival of the three days upon one of which might be expected the cry of the couriers: "The Nile is rising! The Nile is rising! We bring tidings from Meroë!"

Meanwhile, in the land of Goshen, there went out men and women who poured into the ears of the Hebrew people the assurance that the dawning of their liberty was at hand. At no other moment since the coming of the messengers from God among them, and the first awakening of a hope for deliverance, had the Hebrews been so ready to believe as they were in the days following

the disappearance of that awe-inspiring darkness
from which they were so miraculously preserved.
Therein they saw the hand of a Mighty King, a
God of immeasurable power; and when the elders
of their tribes went out, and bade the people look
back to the covenant and promise made with
Abraham, they found willing listeners. Thus it
came that among the Hebrews there was also
activity, but not in the harvesting. They were
preparing for the journey which they were
assured was soon to begin.

Martiesen visited Zoan, and went among the
people over whom he was a ruler, cautioning
prudence and obedience to the government. He
enforced no harsh measures, and when the elders
of the tribes counseled with him, he frankly told
them that he feared the king would send his army
into Goshen to exterminate the Hebrew race.
Meneptah sent orders to establish a most careful
watch over all the territory occupied by the
Hebrews, and Martiesen was directed to dispatch
daily letters to Rameses, giving full details concerning whatever might have been discovered.
To accomplish this more readily, and to make
sure that the Egyptian soldiers under his command did not overstep the instructions, the adon

decided to occupy the headquarters at Zoan in person, and, with Panas and Bariet to second his efforts, he was able to avert much of the hardship which the Pharaoh intended to impose upon the people against whom his anger was so fiercely and unreasonably kindled.

Serah had taken up her abode in the home of Elisheba, but her mother was absent. Scarcely pausing for rest and refreshment, when she learned of the escape of Peshala, Masarah provided herself with the materials necessary to ply her vocation of sorcery, and departed in the direction of Rameses.

Elisheba constantly mingled with her people, and from morning till night was employed in giving instruction and advice to the women. She learned from her father that the Hebrews were about to quit Egypt for all time, and she realized that the poor slaves, who had sprung from generations of bondmen, were like children in their knowledge, and unless organized into orderly companies would become bewildered and panic-stricken when once the start was made. Enlisting the aid of Serah, and acting under the direction of Martiesen and Panas, she toiled early and late, forming divisions under the strongest and most intelligent of the women and superintending preparations to mitigate as far as possible the privations that must come when the homes were left behind. Twice she saw the great prophets, or leaders, and by them her efforts were commended, and she was given instructions how best to continue her work. It was upon an evening following one of these meetings that she met Martiesen at her father's house. They sat upon the roof, apart from the others, and talked long and earnestly of the strange conditions surrounding them.

"The patriarchs have been told by our God that a punishment more terrible than any yet given will be dealt the Egyptians," she said to him, "and they know that the day is not far distant when the Pharaoh will not only release the Hebrews, but will urge their departure."

"And that means, Elisheba, that you go with your people?" he asked.

The girl bowed her head. "Yes, my lord, I shall go with my people — with my father and sisters."

"The danger is great," he said after a moment's reflection. "The Hebrews are a mighty body, for when they were numbered at the king's command, we found there were more than six hundred thousand men, with all their women and children. There is no preparation to sustain them by the wayside. I have moved with armies, and know that careful arrangements must be made to provide large forces with food and water. Even then, when hundreds of slaves are detailed to this work under the orders of a trained commissary, which has the granaries of Egypt to draw upon, the suffering is often severe. And yet it appears that Moses has given this no thought. Can it be possible that he intends to lead this host out into the Arabian wilderness without preparation as to how they shall be fed, or clothed, or where they shall lie?"

"But God has bidden him do it."

"Aye, that may be true; but can the Hebrew God feed these legions of helpless people? How can it be done, when the country into which they journey affords no forage?"

"The God who changes the waters of Egypt into blood and her days into the blackest night, may do even that which you have asked, Martiesen."

This was ever Elisheba's answer when the adon expressed doubts or fears, and her faith was so complete, and so truthfully mirrored the faith of

the thousands with whom he was now almost constantly associated, that Martiesen unconsciously
imbibed much of the same belief. He remained
silent for a moment before he made reply.

"It is so unnecessary," he said. "This land is
broad enough for all, and the Hebrews might
dwell here in happiness, a strength to Egypt, if
the king would only see. By many messages I have
urged this course, and of late I have frequently
begged an audience; but the king's reply has been
that I shall keep the Hebrews in check, and see
that they do not rise suddenly and depart from
the country. Though it is not probable that he
will exact the performance of the tasks until after
the inundation, he will listen to no proposals for
conciliatory measures. As to an audience, I am
forbidden to visit Rameses, or, rather, to cease
my watch upon the Hebrews for a single day; for
Meneptah professes to believe that these poor
serfs are on the eve of revolt."

"Martiesen, why do you not make peace with
your king, and carry out his commands to the
letter? You should not permit your espousal of
the Hebrew cause to prove your undoing."

"Elisheba —— "

"Nay, hear me, my lord. It were better for you

to do this, as I have said. You are of noble birth, and your possessions entitle you to a place with the highest in Egypt. Alone and unaided, you cannot change the course that has been laid down for these two nations, and if you do not cease your opposition to the king, you must fall under his displeasure, which means death, or, what is worse than death, slavery in the mines. I urge you, my lord, to execute what the king has ordered, in spirit and in letter, and to take no further thought of the people of Goshen. It can only be a few days at the most, for the prophets declared today that the final blow was impending. Therefore put aside the promptings of humanity, which stir your nature, and, stifling that love for me which you say throbs in your heart, remain a favorite of the Pharaoh, in peaceful possession of your lands and treasure — an adon and a lord in Egypt."

"Elisheba, do you know what this is that you ask of me?"

"Aye, my lord, I ask you to save yourself from the displeasure and anger of the king."

"And is it because you believe the king worthy of the sacrifice of every generous impulse? Or is it — O happy thought! — because you love me, and would not see me suffer? Speak, Elisheba!"

"It is because I love you, Martiesen," she replied, looking straight in his eyes, "and I would not see you stripped of your place by the king, or burdened with the sufferings of those who go hence to become wanderers."

"Then know, Elisheba, what this king whom you have bidden me obey, has ordered. I have it here, the papyrus he sent two days ago," and the adon drew the roll from his tunic. "In this I am commanded by Meneptah to send you and your cousin Serah prisoners to Rameses, under guard of soldiers named in the papyrus."

The girl rose quickly to her feet, as for flight, then paused beside him as though changed to marble, her face turned appealingly toward the star-lit sky, and her lips parted in affright. Then a convulsive shiver ran through her body, and she crouched against the parapet for support.

"The penalty, Martiesen — the penalty if you fail?" she whispered.

"Ah, Elisheba, any penalty which the cunning of all the priests of the Pharaoh could suggest would be as nothing when weighed against a wrong like this which he commands."

Lower she crouched, and covered her blanched

face with trembling hands. She moaned as one in pain, and her breath came in short, distressing gasps.

"Peshala!" she said. "It is the work of Peshala. He has approached the Pharaoh, as he declared he would."

"I think so, Elisheba, for the soldiers named in this order are men with whom the Libyan was intimate."

Like a poor beast driven to bay, with savage dogs leaping at its throat and eager men urging them on, she cast one hunted, startled glance around, seeking an avenue of escape. But in a moment she was calm, and turned to her lover with a quiet air.

"My lord adon, my cousin Serah and myself are women of a nation held in bondage, and are but the chattels of the king. Yet we would welcome death — for I know the heart of Serah as my own — before we would accept the fate which falls to us, if we go hence upon the order of the Pharaoh. Before we are given over to his guard, I pray you will provide each with a potion, which, when we have started, we may secretly swallow, and die in the hands of our captors before we come to dishonor."

"Stop, Elisheba! Have no such thought as this.

The answer to Meneptah was returned by the messengers who came hither with the demand. Were he thrice the Pharaoh of Egypt, and able to multiply his penalties a thousand times, the answer would still be the same. I will not surrender you into his hands. I have counseled with Panas, and we have planned that you and Serah must leave here tonight, and go out among your people, where it will be possible for you to remain in safety. In such disguises as Serah can invent, you will be secure from detection."

"But, Martiesen, with the knowledge that you are in danger, I cannot go away from Zoan, neither would Serah accompany me, if Panas be in peril."

"You may banish your fears, Elisheba. Panas and I will be watchful, and if necessity compels, we will join with the Hebrews and take refuge in distant settlements. Then, if this to which your elders are daily looking forward should come to pass, our freedom from the wrath of the king may be secured in the same hour in which your people go up out of bondage."

"But the sacrifice, Martiesen. You do not permit yourself to think of all that you must lay aside if you do this. It is not expected, my lord, that the high and noble shall look with compassion upon those who are so far beneath them."

"Ah, Elisheba, I have learned something that is not taught in the temples of our many gods. It is this: To guard the virtue and preserve the happiness of woman is the noblest act in which man may engage, and to this end no sacrifice is too great. And if it should fall out that in so doing the man may win the woman's love and keep it to himself alone, then it is a richer reward than the gods are able to bestow. With that I shall be content."

She was about to reply, when Panas, speaking from the ground, attracted the adon's attention.

"My lord," said the lieutenant in a low tone, "two galleys filled with armed men approach the landing."

"Have you a guard, Panas?"

"Ten men, my lord."

"Station them at this house, under Bariet, and meet the galleys at the landing in person. Inform the commander that I await him at headquarters, and draw a suitable escort from the garrison to conduct him thither. Let your men fraternize with the newcomers, and keep them in a pleasant mood. Above all, be ready for immediate action, if it becomes necessary for us to resist."

Martiesen turned to Elisheba, who scarcely

comprehended the importance of the communication made by the lieutenant. "The king has not delayed," he said, "for his soldiers are at hand, it may be to enforce the order I refused to obey. I did not expect them before the evening of the morrow, but I am not unprepared. Explain to your father and Serah what is needful, and be ready to depart with the utmost secrecy at any moment. Either Panas or Bariet will bear my message."

He descended the stairway, and was passing hurriedly through the lower room, when the door was darkened, and a woman's voice spoke his name.

"Masarah!" he said in astonishment. "Your arrival is indeed opportune. When did you return?"

"This moment, my lord, scarcely in advance of two galleys now approaching the landing and carrying soldiers."

"Panas has informed me of their coming. By whom are they commanded?"

"Peshala, the Libyan, and Totoes, the outcast priest!"

The adon started, and laid his hand on his sword.

"What warrant do they bear?"

"That I cannot say, my lord. I watched them several days in Rameses, and endeavored to learn how far they have influenced the king, if, indeed, they secured audience with him at all. They were often at the temple, in consultation with the priests, and I think they have received assistance in their plans from that source, for yesterday, when they came from the small pylon, they were laughing, and after that they had money. Peshala also consulted with the ab, who is not a friend to either the Hebrews or yourself, and this leads me to fear that their errand is directed against you."

"Pray the gods that it may be no other. What soldiers do they bring? "

"Two companies."

"Aye, but of what force?"

"I could not ascertain, but this I was told, that Peshala was commissioned to employ a force to come to Zoan for prisoners of state."

"Then they are not of the king's companies?"

"They are trained soldiers, my lord, who at the present time were at their homes on the yearly furlough. I could not resort to the streets freely, my lord, for it was known after the arrival of Totoes and Peshala that they were seeking a certain soothsayer named Masarah and her daughter Serah. I secured asylum in the house of a merchant, Nodes by name, whose daughter, through the use of gold I gave her, escaped from Manhotef the very night that your departure caused such confusion. She knew me as I passed her father's house, and running down from the balcony brought me within. Nodes concealed me in his store-room, and being a man of intelligence, procured for me all the information I have given you."

"Masarah, you are weary with your journey, but you have done priceless service for me and for those you love. I know not what I am to meet, but what you tell me, gives me knowledge that may be of great value in deciding my course. Provide yourself with refreshment, and then see that Elisheba and Serah are disguised in the habit of the women who work in the fields. They will tell you why. Hold them ready for instant departure, if word comes from either Panas or myself that swift measures are necessary."

CHAPTER XIX

THE SIGNATURE OF THE PHAROAH

Two Egyptian companies had long been employed as a garrison at Zoan, and these were quartered in a low brick building not far from the landing-place. The adon was required to hold a certain part of this force at the garrison at all times, and to keep small detachments of the remainder of his command moving throughout the section occupied by the Hebrews, thus constantly reminding those held in bondage, that revolt, or failure to comply with the demands of the taskmasters, would be met with punishment. A number of these soldiers had taken wives among the Hebrews, and through this means were led, to a considerable degree, to espouse the Hebrew cause. Indeed, there was never any friction between the military and the Hebrews. The soldiers met obedience and kindness from these people, and they learned that the Hebrews were unlike the slaves or captives brought from the nations against which Egypt made war. Thus, even in the dull minds of men trained from infancy for the military class, there grew up a sympathy for those whom they were sent to keep under subjection. No doubt the common soldiers were largely influenced in this by Martiesen and Panas, who at all times displayed humane qualities quite unusual in the men of that era who held others at their mercy. Moreover, since the appearance of the plagues, the soldiers had lost much of their fear of the king, for when they saw that he was utterly powerless to cope with the mysterious force that fought the battle for the Hebrews, their belief was shattered as to the invincibility of the occupant of the Egyptian throne.

All this was well known to Martiesen, and he considered it as he ran over in his mind the avenues open to him.

He had no thought of surrendering Elisheba and Serah to Peshala; nor would he submit to the indignity and danger of an arrest at the hands of those approaching, no matter whose commission they bore. If the king commanded his appearance at Rameses, he would obey; but he would proceed thither in his own barge, and under his own guard, and take care that his friends were warned of his journey, that they might rally to his support. Should an attempt be made to compel any other course, he would resist with those under his command. Not more than one company of his troops was at present in Zoan, but several bands of Hebrews were armed with a few crude weapons, and these could be brought to his immediate assistance.

Still, the adon desired to avoid an open rupture if possible, for this would be a firebrand to the king's anger, and would precipitate an attack. Within a few hours an army of the Pharaoh's charioteers, spear-men, archers, lancers, and axemen would be hurled upon the almost wholly defenseless people of Goshen, and there would ensue a massacre that would sweep the Hebrews from the face of the earth. Nor did Martiesen doubt that the opportunity of doing this would be hailed with satisfaction by Meneptah, for there had recently come to his ears fresh confirmations of the story that the king was considering the utter extinction of the descendants of Israel.

In the garrison building there was one large room for general assemblage, several smaller rooms for offices and accoutrements, and an executive department for the use of the commanding officer. To this Martiesen repaired immediately. The room was bare of ornament or furniture, except such as pertained to military life, and upon reaching it the adon at once gave attention to some of the details of his command. Summoning his scribe, the adon dictated several minor reports and orders, and while these were being prepared for his inspection, he took from his belt the order directing him to send Elisheba and Serah as prisoners to Rameses. Placing it before him on the table, he began a more careful perusal of the document than he had heretofore given it. He had not proceeded beyond the customary greeting, when the scribe, Bailos, approached to make inquiries concerning some of the calculations, and together their heads bent over the figures. The scribe's hand accidentally rested upon the papyrus which the adon was examining when interrupted. He raised his head suddenly, took the papyrus between his thumb and finger, and carefully felt its texture. Martiesen looked at him inquiringly.

"What is it, Bailos?" he asked.

"From the priest of Manhotef, he that is called Totoes, king of the ruins," was the reply.

"The scroll? No, it is from Rameses, the order of the Pharaoh, which came to me two days ago while you were absent at the villa."

Bailos bent over the papyrus for a closer examination, and after making a careful inspection, shook his head incredulously.

"It is very strange, my lord, but this is from the papyrus grown upon the marshes back of the ruined city of Manhotef. It is unlike any other in Egypt, because of a quality in the soil peculiar to that locality. It is known to all scribes who have served in the office of the ab, to whom Totoes writes numerous memorials, seeking to regain his standing."

The adon took the roll in his hands, and gave it his closest scrutiny.

"If my lord adon will compare it with other papyrus, he will see that it is of coarser grain, and not nearly so pliable in fiber as that commonly used." And the scribe brought several pieces for his comparison.

"It is true as you say, Bailos. But the writing and the cartouche? Is not the signature of our ruler so sacred that it may not be made even by the ab, except in the king's presence?"

The scribe unrolled the papyrus, and studied the hieroglyphics with minutest care. "It is not the writing of a practiced scribe, my lord, unless he has purposely disguised his characters, and this the scribes of the ab would not have reason for doing. The cartouche is bold and strong, but it was made by neither the Pharaoh nor the ab, for the ink has been laid on with careful strokes, as by one who follows a copy. Nor is the ink from that used in the royal palace, its shade is not so black."

"The wrappings, Bailos! Search the refuse for the wrappings!"

Bailos entered a small anteroom at the right, and while he was absent, the adon procured several documents which he knew to be genuine, and compared them with the one under suspicion. He was thus engaged when Bailos returned with the bands of linen which were bound about the roll when it was received, and to these their united attention was at once directed.

"See, my lord," said the scribe, presently, "these wrappings have done service before, for here they have been severed and again cleverly fastened together. Nor is the wax of the seals as fresh as it should be, for it is hardened, as though by an exposure of several weeks. The document is a forgery."

CHAPTER XX

THE PENALTY FOR COUNTERFEITING

A CHALLENGE by a sentry at the entrance of the assembly-room and the giving of a password interrupted further conversation. There was the sound of marching men, and the adon had scarcely time to roll the papyrus and conceal it in his robe before Panas entered. In precise, military terms the lieutenant made known the arrival of those who claimed audience with the governor of the nome upon business of such importance that it would admit of no delay. Martiesen stepped through the doorway, and there saw, in the center of the assembly-room, Peshala in the uniform of a captain, Totoes by his side in the half-frock of a priest, and near them, in double rank, about a score of soldiers. A quick glance told the adon that back of these stood a file drawn from his own command, and he doubted not that they were ready to do his bidding, whatever it might be.

"Upon what urgent business do you request audience, at this hour, with the governor of the Nome of the Prince?" he demanded, but without acknowledging the salute with which Peshala and those accompanying him greeted the adon's entrance.

The Libyan, disconcerted by the question and the manner of reception, hesitated an instant before making answer, but, recovering himself, he replied: "We come at the command of Meneptah, the Pharaoh and Ruler of Lower and Upper Egypt, Wearer of two crowns, Lord of all this land, and of the people —— "

"I know the titles you would name," interrupted the adon, "and respect them all. Let that suffice, and disclose to me what I seek to learn — the errand which brings the Libyan scribe and an outcast priest before me."

"Then let your ears drink the knowledge at once," replied Peshala, with spirit. "It is to arrest the adon Martiesen and convey him to Rameses, there to meet charges which declare that he has entered upon conspiracies threatening the welfare of the state and the peaceful rule of its lawful king. I bear the warrant."

He stepped forward to display the warrant, but the adon stopped him with a sweep of his arm.

"If the king commands," he said with marked distinctness, so that no word might be lost upon the soldiers before him, "I will repair to Rameses at once, and in the manner befitting my station. It is well known in the armies of Egypt that Martiesen has never been unmindful of his duty to his ruler; but I refuse to receive at the hands of forgers a warrant purporting to come from the mighty Meneptah, believing that the document may be as spurious as one which preceded it two days past."

"Forgers, my lord adon!" exclaimed the priest. "Ho, ho! a pretty tale to flaunt in the face of true messengers of the king, who at midday, in the presence of his court, set his cartouche upon the warrant, and then gave it into the hands of the ab, that it might be delivered to his captain, Peshala, for execution."

"Your story, priest, may be no more truthful than those you told me in Manhotef. I recall them with doubts as to your present honesty of speech. But tell me, did Meneptah, the Pharaoh whom you and Peshala profess to honor and serve faithfully, set his hand to this document, commanding that two Hebrew women in the instrument named be sent to Rameses as prisoners?" And the adon held the papyrus roll above his head.

The priest glanced at Peshala, expecting him to answer, but the Libyan stood with blanched cheeks, and from his trembling lips there came no reply.

"If it bears the king's cartouche, my lord, he authorized it," replied the priest, "for none would dare counterfeit the signature of the mighty lord of Egypt, whose name may be spoken only in awe — the ruler at whose summons all offenders must tremble, Meneptah, the Pharaoh."

"Tell me, Totoes, what is the penalty for counterfeiting the signature of Meneptah, Lord and Ruler of Lower and Upper Egypt?"

"There is no need to repeat it," replied Totoes, with assumed indifference, "when every boy in Egypt knows how it is written."

"But speak it, for yourself and your commander, that those in this room may know if you have learned your lesson well."

All eyes were turned upon the unwilling priest, and a moment of most intense and painful silence ensued before his words came.

"It is written in the law," he said very slowly and in a low voice, "that the fingernails of one who forges the king's cartouche shall be plucked out, one each day, until the hands are cleared. The two succeeding days the sight of the eyes shall be destroyed; and then, if the malefactor survives, he shall be exposed to the populace. On the next day he shall be beheaded."

"Soldiers of Meneptah, you have heard what Totoes, the outcast priest of Manhotef, has said, and you know that he repeats the law as it is written. I, Martiesen, adon of the Nome of the Prince, a lord in Egypt, in whose veins runs the blood of your kings, command you to seize this Totoes and his confederate Peshala, upon a charge of counterfeiting the cartouche of the Pharaoh. Here is the false signature, and I will lay it before the king as a witness."

Martiesen spoke with such convincing force, and the soldiers were so accustomed to obey those who commanded by the authority of blood, that the guard accompanying Peshala moved forward in company with the adon's force to do his bidding. With a bound, Totoes leaped against the soldier nearest him, and sent the man sprawling on the floor. Dealing another a blow across the face with a sword which he brought from under his frock, the priest shouted to Peshala, and with backs together and swords flashing, they fought their way towards the door. Panas sprang forward and engaged the priest, and the adon sought a similar encounter with Peshala, but the soldiers crowded him aside in their eagerness, and set upon the agile pair with clumsy weapons and unskillful movements. The priest was more than a match for Panas, and soon the lieutenant's sword went clattering to the floor. Before it could be recovered, or anyone interpose, the priest dealt a blow that sent Panas down upon his knees, stunned and bleeding. Several of the soldiers were by this time wounded by the vigorous strokes of Peshala, and the guardsmen became more cautious in their attack.

Realizing that the escape of both was imminent, the adon took up the fight for Panas, and the moment his sword flashed against that of Totoes, the priest felt that his doom was sealed. But death with the hot blood leaping, and with the clash of steel and shouts of men in his ears, and the waving of torches before his eyes, was far better than to suffer the torture due to a counterfeiter. With this thought the priest lunged forward, showing a strength and determination that promised success for the moment. Left alone by this movement, Peshala was quickly overpowered and bound. Lying there upon the floor, a bruised and beaten prisoner, he watched with varying emotions of hope and fear the struggle which none attempted to interrupt.

Martiesen had the advantage of youth; but this was matched by a better knowledge of sword-play, longer practice, and tougher sinews on the part of Totoes. Both fought with the valor of desperation, each realized that more than life depended on the result. Time and again the vantage turned, and those who, spellbound, stood with bated breath and watched each change in the rapidly-shifting scene, were lost in wonder that the clashing blades of polished bronze did not reach the flesh toward which they leaped like tongues of gleaming fire. Blow upon blow was turned aside with ready parry, while eager thrusts went harmless past the points at which they aimed.

But youth triumphs in a test of endurance and strength. The priest's lips were drawn back from his teeth, his eyes grew dim from the intensity of the exertion, and his breath came in quick and painful gasps, which did not fill his heaving chest or cool his heated blood. Slowly he was forced back to a corner of the room, each moment offering less intrepid defense.

"Down, Totoes! down and yield yourself a prisoner!" roared the deep voices of the soldiers, as the ringing strokes grew slower, and the adon held his antagonist at his mercy.

The shout aroused his fading energy. A prisoner! Totoes a prisoner, to be turned over to the executioners! Totoes, the king of Manhotef, who ruled his wretches with a tyrant's hand, a prisoner?

"Never!" he cried in desperate rage, and nerved himself anew to strike with greater vigor. In a crash his blade flew spinning from his hand, but with successful effort he leaped aside and avoided the adon's thrust. Quickly he bent low, and darting to Martiesen's side, wrenched the Libyan dagger from its sheath. There was a shout of triumph from Peshala, and those looking on saw a gleam of light as Totoes raised his hand to strike. But before the blow could fall, Martiesen with a mighty stroke sent his blade straight through the breast of the priest of Manhotef.

Staggering backward with outstretched arms, Totoes stood a moment, the bronze blade piercing his body. Then, as approaching death drew its veil over his eyes, and with a scream of vengeance on his foam-covered lips, he lunged blindly forward in the agony of his supreme moment, striking right and left for a victim to his frenzied passion. The hardened men of warfare fell back in consternation from a sight more horrible and appalling than any their eyes had ever beheld, and stood against the entrance way, fascinated by terror. Martiesen saw the danger, and catching the half-conscious Panas from the corner toward which the priest was staggering, dodged the blows which cleft the air with lightning-like rapidity, and bore the lieutenant to the anteroom. A wail, a cry of fearful agony, a piercing scream for aid arose from the bound and helpless Peshala, lying there where they had left him. Yet no man dared stretch forth a hand to save.

Reeling, almost falling backward, with the death-rattle in his throat and a film closing upon his eyes, Totoes stumbled, crawled upon his knees a pace or two, then struck with all his fading strength. Then he raised the dripping blade and struck again, and yet again, and then fell down upon that which he struck.

And the life-blood of Totoes and Peshala ran together on the rough-tiled floor.

∩∩|

CHAPTER XXI

THE SENTENCE

ON the morning succeeding the events chron-
icled in the preceding chapter, the adon Martiesen ordered the re-embarkation of the force
which Totoes and Peshala had led to Zoan, and
with a large retinue of his own soldiers he
proceeded to Manhotef. It was there learned that
Peshala had appeared at the ruined place while
the people were still searching for their leader.
Heading a party of picked men, the scribe pene-
trated to the tomb, released the priest and his
companions, and from them he heard the story of
Masarah's part in aiding the adon to escape. That
the counterfeit order of the Pharaoh commanding the presence of the two Hebrew girls in
Rameses had been written at Manhotef was also
made certain, for the two fellows were found who

were disguised as messengers of the king, and sent with the papyrus to Zoan. The Libyan had named certain soldiers in the order to accompany Elisheba and Serah as a guard to Rameses, expecting that he would prevail upon them to land at Manhotef, as they were men over whom he had some influence. The return of the messengers bearing the firm but respectful reply of the adon declining to send the Hebrew women, was a great surprise to the plotters, for they had no thought that the adon would have the courage to refuse point blank an order that apparently emanated from the Pharaoh. As the plan had failed, however, it would not do to wait, and so Peshala and Totoes left at once for Rameses.

Upon hearing these facts, the adon compelled the false messengers to accompany him, and he continued his journey to the capital. At first he was denied audience with the king, but certain powerful princes, who were put in possession of some part of the story, intervened to bring about a meeting between the adon and the ruler. The adon gave an account of the events immediately leading up to the death of Totoes and Peshala, and presented the evidence of their guilt. He was informed that the order for his arrest was made upon representation of the plotters, that he was inciting sedition, if he was not in full conspiracy against the throne. The Libyan had solemnly declared, that if he were put in charge of the expedition to arrest Martiesen, he would be able to secure and bring the king evidence proving the existence of a widespread plot. He was therefore given a commission to execute the warrant.

Moved to intense anger by the discovery that the informers had forged his signature, the king dismissed as false all the statements made by them concerning treasonable acts on the part of Martiesen. He reminded the adon that his family had long been loyal and trusted, and chided him sharply for his insistent requests that the policy of the government be changed toward the Hebrews. Thus purged of suspicion, the adon was permitted to return at once to his villa.

Within the next few days Martiesen was visited by several of the princes, who urged that the plan to seize the government should not be abandoned, for the time was now more favorable to such a step than it had been previous to the plague of darkness. He learned that over all Lower and Middle Egypt there was great discontent. The tax-collectors, who went abroad at the

time of the ingathering, found it almost impossible to secure the tithes, and though they
beat the people unmercifully, the grain was not
forthcoming, because it had been destroyed by
the plagues. Tidings of the coming of the inundation were delayed beyond the customary time,
and this was another reason for discontent and
fear. All the Egyptian plain lay panting in the
burning sun. Dust, and age, and drought covered
the land and turned it to ashes. The ground was
cracked by the heat, and every breeze sent
whirling clouds of sand high into the air, but still
the message did not come that Father Nile had
awakened from his sleep. Had the God of the
Hebrews held back the waters as a further punishment upon the king?

This question was by no means confined to the
agriculturalist and artisan, but was running
through the military forces, and was asked in the
homes of the nobles. It was upon every tongue, it
pervaded every assemblage. Under their breath,
men asked why those in the highest places did not
propitiate the Hebrew God, and thus release their
stricken land from the blight under which it had
been struggling these many months. Those who
came to Martiesen told him this, and, pledging

him their support, they urged that he raise his standard.

But Martiesen hesitated. Like all the others, he had an indefinable consciousness of the approach of a great calamity. Try as he might, he could not bring himself to consider seriously the counsel of his visitors. One after another — for they came singly or in pairs, and without pomp or show — he dismissed them with the promise that soon, very soon, he would make another appeal to the king, and if that failed, he would act.

And still the dread and unrest grew. The adon knew it extended to all the Hebrew hosts; but none there could tell him aught. Moses — grand, mysterious, silent, as befitted one who held the friendship and confidence of God — came among his people daily, and to the men whom he had chosen as leaders gave brief commands hastening forward the preparations commenced on the dawn of the day that broke the plague of darkness. Moses bandied no words. "Thus saith the Lord," he declared, and when God's words had been spoken, the leader added none of his own. "Do this," commanded the austere master, who came to them so mysteriously, and brought in his hands a power greater than that of the mighty king who enslaved them; and the poor slaves who heard, laid aside fear of every other master, and hastened to obey his bidding. The promise of liberty and the prophecy of greatness for their nation fell upon ears that did not appreciate what was meant, and these promises and prophecies alone would not have stirred to action a people long stunted and dwarfed by servility to an idolatrous and tyrannical court. It required all the marvels and punishments that had been shown them, to awaken the nearly extinct greatness which was to burst forth again in future generations.

Aye, and it required one to come — that fearful visit of Death now casting its shadow into every heart.

At last there came to the elders of the Hebrew tribes a strange, new command. In every household a lamb without blemish should be chosen, and in the evening of a certain day it must be slain. The blood, caught in a basin, should be taken to the doorways, and there with bunches of hyssop it should be sprinkled upon the lintel and doorposts of the entrance. Then with loins girded, staff in hand, and sandals fastened to their feet, they must eat of the roasted flesh, and permit no part to remain unconsumed. All through Goshen, in Zoan and Pithom, in Rameses, in the villages and huts wherever a Hebrew dwelt, ran messengers to spread this command of a God whom they had not learned to love, but whom with trembling and with fear they obeyed.

Darda was among those present when the prophet gave to the elders the words of God, and upon him devolved the duty of taking the command to the masses in Zoan. Scarcely resting day or night, he passed from house to house, guiding, counseling, and instructing his people, that they might perform this new rite in strict accordance with the law, and thus escape the penalty sure to fall upon those who, either willfully or in ignorance, neglected to keep the feast. Toward the evening of the day designated, he approached his own home, conscious that his work had been faithfully performed. Summoning his daughters and Masarah and Serah, he directed that preparations should be made for the feast, for the hour was near at hand when they would start toward the land of new promise.

"This night," he said, "there shall come upon the house of Pharaoh, and to every house in

Egypt that does not set up the token commanded of God, the most fearful punishment that has yet been dealt to this land. For at midnight a Destroying Angel will pass through, and from the highest to the lowest, in every house upon the lintel and doorposts of which the blood of a lamb has not been sprinkled, the firstborn must die."

At first they did not fully realize the tremendous import of the sentence. They were accustomed to war and bloodshed, for the Egyptian king led his armies into many countries, and tales of battle and conquest were upon the lips of every soldier. But of vengeance such as this they had not heard, nor could they bring themselves to think it true. But grave Darda sat before them with bowed head, and well they knew he was not the man to jest. Slowly the truth took root, and when full realization came, the women looked into each others' faces, silent, appalled, stricken with horror. It was as if the Master of Death stood there beside them, with hand half-poised, waiting their election, whether in that house he should find a victim.

With a moan Elisheba leaped to her feet, and struck her hand upon her forehead.

"Father, father! Do I hear aright? May none of

the firstborn of the Egyptians escape from this sentence pronounced by our God?"

Darda looked with compassion upon his daughter, and shook his head in reply.

"Martiesen!"

They saw the name form upon her lips, but fear and horror kept its sound below her breath.

Darda did not make answer, but bent his head in sorrow. This thought had come to him several days before, that the young adon was the first-born of his father's house, and it was a heavy burden upon his heart, for he loved Martiesen as a son.

"Masarah! Serah! Father! Tell me what I may do to save his life! Surely the God of the Hebrews does not know of Martiesen's kindness to the enslaved people, and of all he has suffered in their behalf. Go, my father, go to the prophet and tell him all! Aye, and take me with you that we may ask, and beg, and plead, that from the house of Martiesen the shaft shall be turned away!"

She was upon the floor beside her father, pulling at his robe and clasping her hands about his neck, entreating him with impassioned words and quick caress to interpose, to raise his voice in protest, to help her fight against the doom fast gathering about her lover.

"Nay, Elisheba," said her father, with gentleness, "it may not be. The prophet Moses is far away, at Succoth, preparing to lead our people forth on the morrow, for with this mighty stroke our shackles will be broken, and Israel will be thrust out of Egypt. We must obey the command, lest upon ourselves the punishment be visited."

She arose from the floor, white, calm, determined, and stood a moment before her father in earnest thought.

"Then will I welcome that punishment, and here in Egypt I will sleep in happiness, because he whom I love rests in the same land."

The aged Darda raised his hand in protest.

"My father, because you were given no sons, all your affection has been poured out upon me, and I have been as your right hand, and out of my love have obeyed your slightest wish. But I cannot follow you to this land of promise, while my heart is buried here. Kill the lamb as God has commanded, and strike the blood upon the lintel and the doorposts, that nothing may be omitted from the rite. To me, as I stand without, give some little portion of the blood in a basin, and with it I will hasten to the home of Martiesen, to set the mark above the door, hoping that when the angel shall see the sign, he will know that within lies one who has befriended this enslaved people, even to the hazard of his life. But should the Destroyer not pass by, then I, who will have crept within the portico, will meet him there, and beg this messenger of God to slay me with the stroke that kills Martiesen."

So full of saddened tenderness was her voice, and yet so determined her manner, that those who stood about were awed to a silence that was not broken until Darda spoke.

"You love him thus, my daughter?"

"Aye, more than this I love Martiesen! For, had I many lives, and could I spend each in suffering throughout all its natural years, and thus save him one moment's sorrow, it should be done. Even more than this I love Martiesen! For the command of my father, who in all my life I have not disobeyed in the slightest particular, would not now turn me from this purpose."

Darda arose, and clasped her in his arms. He held her close against his breast a few moments, and half releasing her gazed into her eyes.

"Go, my daughter," he said in deepest tender-ness, "and through the night I will bow in supplication to the God of Abraham, Isaac, and Jacob for your safety and the safety of Martiesen, your lover."

Serah came to them with mute sympathy, and, taking Elisheba's hands, drew them to her bosom, and covered them with tears.

"Nay, Serah, do not weep," said Elisheba. "Go with my father, and be his eldest daughter. Panas, whom you love so dearly, escapes this sentence, and is here in Zoan, ready to join the hosts when they march forth tomorrow. Take him to your household, my father, and if I come not again to your side, the strong arms of Panas and the loving care of Serah will protect and lighten your declining years. If I may save Martiesen's life, then will I return and go hence with my people, happy and content in knowing that he lives; but if he, too, falls under the sentence, then Egypt will remain my desolate home."

CHAPTER XXII

THE FIRSTBORN

As the evening deepened into night, the home of Martiesen was in peaceful rest. Cares and duties were laid aside, and, with the exception of the master himself, the household slept. The adon remained in the salon, sometimes pacing the tiled floor, but more frequently reclining upon a light rattan couch, which had been drawn near the windows for greater comfort. A few hours previously two princes of the blood, who came like others with an appeal on their lips, that he would consent to lead a revolt, had departed from the villa, and now the adon was for the hundredth time considering the subject of their conversation. Could he save Egypt? Could he do aught to hold the Hebrews within her borders and make them a strength to Egypt? These were the questions around which his thoughts centered. The adon well knew that revolution frequently succeeded, and he felt that at this time the chances for success were strong. He went over them carefully, and noted each with satisfaction, until he came to reckon with this unknown, mysterious Hebrew Deity, who seemed to baffle all plans and set at defiance every law of nature. How could he hope to succeed, if this strange force should not be with him? Then he made up his mind to seek Moses and Aaron, and ask them plainly if such a course would be pleasing to the God whose words they spoke. But to do this was difficult. The prophets would appear suddenly in Rameses, and boldly declare to the king the command of God; then they would disappear as suddenly as they came, and for weeks no tidings would be heard from them. Darda might give him assistance in meeting them, he thought, and this led him to the decision that on the morrow, in Zoan, he would ask the aged Hebrew's aid.

And with this his thoughts turned to Elisheba, queenly, beautiful, yet modest Elisheba, who had displayed so much courage throughout all the perils into which she had been thrown, and who would willingly have sacrificed her life rather than see him lose his caste. There came to him the memory of the smile she wore when she noted his approach, and its beauty was like nothing else he had ever beheld. He heard her low voice and laughter, and they were sweeter than any music his ears had ever caught. Thinking thus, he forgot the throne of Egypt, and all the pomp and power it would bring, and, as he fell asleep, he dreamed only of domestic scenes, of love and happiness, with Elisheba by his side.

The night was close and murky. In any other country one would have said that the still, lifeless atmosphere betokened an oncoming storm; but here in Egypt there was no thought of this. The days and nights preceding the rising of the Nile are hot and listless, save for the wind which blows for fifty days ever from the south. Occasionally the distant beating of the oars of a belated boatman could be heard, and once the low crooning of a woman to her baby came indistinctly over the water. Her husband, a soldier, sat by her side, and played with the child, their firstborn, which he had never seen until this evening. He had been absent with his company, and when his yearly furlough was due, his wife met him with their baby at Rameses, and now they were hurrying to their home. Ah, before dawn the happy cradle song will be changed to a chant of mourning!

Deeper grew the night, and in its dense shadows a small boat, rowed by a man with one maimed arm, silently and swiftly approached the landing-place. As the boat touched the lower step, a woman arose, and with nervous haste stepped from the craft. She carried in her hands a small vessel, wrapped with extreme care in spotless linen, and with it a bunch of hyssop.

"Moor the boat quickly, Bariet," she said in a low tone, "and come with me, that you may explain my errand to the guard."

"There is no guard, my lady," he replied as he came to her side. "My master is beloved of his people, and therefore sleeps in security."

"Then seek a place where you may rest," she said to him kindly. "That which remains to be done, I must do alone."

"I will stay here, my lady," replied the Assyrian, "where you may find me in a moment if I am wanted."

"If there is need of you, Bariet, it will not be until day. Come to the portico as soon as it is light, and if you find me there, and I am not alive, then return with all speed to Darda, and tell him what you saw; and say that on my face there was a look of happiness. Farewell, Bariet, you have been faithful to your trust."

"My lady, if there is danger —— "

"Nay, Bariet; if there is danger, none may share it with me."

She started forward along the approach, and the Assyrian, wondering, yet silent, watched until her form faded into the shadows of the night. Then he brought a mat from the boat, and composed himself to rest.

The approach leading to the house of the adon was bordered on both sides by a row of small houses, in which resided the attendants and officers attached to his household. Fronting these houses were double rows of dromos and sphinxes, brought hither from ruined temples or cities in the vicinity, or carved upon the spot, at the direction of former governors of the nome.

A broad, paved roadway led straight between these monuments to the portico.

Looking neither to right nor left, almost running, yet stepping with extreme caution, lest she fall, Elisheba made her way in silence to the portico. Carefully unwrapping the linen from the jar, trembling in every limb, and choking back the moans and sobs which anxiety wrung from her heart, she thrust the fragrant hyssop into the vessel. Then, climbing the buttressed columns of the portico to the highest possible point, she leaped outward and upward, and struck upon the glistening marble keystone the scarlet blood of the sacrificial lamb.

She fell heavily to the pavement, but recovering quickly, caught up the vessel, and with the hyssop set the red token upon either side the doorway.

Creeping close within the spacious entrance, crouching against the hinges of the door itself, numbed and bruised by her fall, yet calm and confident that, come life, come death, she would be with Martiesen, Elisheba awaited the midnight hour.

And there was a great cry in Egypt. Into the homes of the king, the counselor, the prince, the priest, the soldier, the artisan, the tax-gatherer, the fisherman, the farmer, the servant, the slave, Death entered, and from the firstborn of Pharaoh that sat on his throne unto the firstborn of the captive that was in the dungeon, none was spared, if upon the lintel and doorposts of their habitation the sign had not been set. They who lived ran into the open air for help, and met there others whose circle had been broken by the same heavy hand. In the populous town or city, in the struggling village, in the lonely houses beside the river or upon the canals; among all the splendor and in the shadows of beautiful monuments and temples; among all the misery and squalor where the poor, mean homes were flanked by the desert or surrounded by ruins — there was none who could go to his neighbor and say, "Thou art in trouble and affliction, whilst I am free. Take thou my sympathy."

Without the customary warnings of old age or disease, in the interval of a breath, that from which all peoples since the dawn of intelligence have shrunk in dread, swept upon Egypt like the flash of a crimson-stained scimitar; and when its stroke passed, there remained in its pathway children bereft of parents, wives mourning for husbands, and husbands mourning for wives, the aged from whom support had been snapped, or lovers in whose ears the love-song had suddenly been turned to a sob.

In all time past or in all time to come, no punishment of a people had been or could be more widespread or terrible.

From the houses of soldiers and servants within the villa of the adon, the alarm was not wanting, first in one where a mother found her child dead beside her; then in another, and another, and another, where a husband was dead, or a mother was stricken, or a daughter's life had gone out, or a son had ceased to breathe, or it may be two were dead, or sometimes more. Torches appeared upon the broad approach, and men, women, and children sprang from their couches in terror, and sought the open air.

"Woe! woe! for Anpu the god of the dead rules the world!"

"He hath broken the bonds set upon him by Osiris! He is abroad with his mighty lance! Woe! woe! woe! for many are dead!"

Shivering in the hot, murky night, choking with grief, dumb or hysterical with the weight of sorrow, they huddled together in the center of the approach, and gazed with horror into each other's blanched and unnatural faces.

Bariet, sleeping on his mat at the landing, was awakened by the cries, and ran toward the gathering, fearing that harm had come to his mistress. Voices broken with sobs answered his questions, but not until he had looked in upon the dead of several homes could he believe what they told him.

"Let us summon the adon," he said in hushed tones, and taking a torch he led the way to the portico. And there, crouching against the door, with no sign of life, he saw Elisheba. With a cry, he dropped the torch, and raised her in his arms. Throwing back the covering of her head and face, he brought her like a baby into the open space, and gazed upon her, mutely and in fear. There was warmth to her body, the breath came faintly from her nostrils, and when he bent his head upon her breast, Bariet could hear the beating of her heart. Anxiety and suspense had brought kindly unconsciousness to her overwrought senses; but the hand of the angel of death had not been laid upon her.

"Make an alarm at the door," commanded Bariet. "Let Martiesen come to give us comfort and advice."

"Aye, Martiesen! Martiesen!" shouted a dozen voices as they pounded the metal tubes, and struck upon the door itself. "Awake, my lord adon, if you be alive! Awake, for the people of your household are in the grasp of Anpu!"

A woman knelt beside Bariet, and chafed

Elisheba's hands and temples. Hot, scalding tears ran down her cheeks, and fell upon the fair young form which she stroked with so much tenderness. But in the flickering lights she saw bloodstains upon the girl's hands, and in an instant all her gentleness was turned to frenzy.

"A witch! A murderous wraith!" she screamed, leaping to her feet. "Here, with the blood of victims on her hands! Avenge, avenge!"

She attempted to strike the girl with a staff which she caught from the pavement, but Bariet warded off the blow with his maimed arm, and sent the woman reeling backward. The crowd deserted the door, and taking up the cry of the woman, rushed upon him; but the Assyrian, with Elisheba in his arms, dodged them in the darkness, and gained the portico. He thrust the girl back of him, where she clung half-conscious to the latch, and then he turned and faced the eager mob.

"She is not a witch," he shouted in their faces, "and is as guiltless as any among you. No hand may touch her with violence while I live."

"Who is she, slave?" demanded one of the captains whom Bariet knew well.

"Elisheba, the daughter of Darda, the Hebrew; and she practices neither magic nor witchcraft."

A flood of light came into the portico, and fell upon the circle of men and women crowded about the entrance. The door leading to the house opened, and upon the doorstep, backed by servants who bore tapers, lamps, and arms, stood the adon.

"Who speaks the name of Elisheba?" he demanded. But there was no need for reply — Elisheba sprang forward, and fell at his feet.

Martiesen bore her in his arms to a couch, and put her in the hands of attendants. Then he came to the portico, and listened with a heavy heart to what Bariet and his people could tell. He returned to the salon, and Elisheba told him that this which had happened at his villa was repeated over the length and breadth of Egypt. With bowed head and trembling lips, he visited the afflicted homes of those attached to his house, and to each wondering mourner — wondering why this heavy hand was laid upon those who were innocent — he told whence the blow had fallen.

CHAPTER XXIII

THE PROMISE

W<small>HEN</small> all that he could do to allay the fears and relieve the sorrows of his afflicted people had been accomplished, Martiesen went back to the salon, where he found Elisheba ready for the return to Zoan.

"Why do you depart so soon, Elisheba?" he asked with solicitude. "You are wearied with this through which you have passed, and should take rest before your return."

"There is no time for rest, my lord. The day will soon break, and with its coming my people are to start upon their journey."

"Today, Elisheba?"

"Aye, my lord, the command was so given. The Hebrews have slept throughout this night with sandals upon their feet and their loins girded, and close by their hands lay their staffs, that nothing might delay their exodus this day, as God has promised."

"I did not think it would be so soon. Nor can it be, Elisheba, for the king has not given permission."

"Whether Meneptah gives consent or not, is now of small matter to the Hebrews, my lord. The time for our going out has come, and can no longer be delayed. Even the Pharaoh cannot withstand his people in the face of this great plague of death, for they will rise from their mourning with the coming of the dawn, and thrust us forth, fearing that if we remain longer, none of them may be left alive."

As if in answer to her words, a commotion was heard in the approach, and Martiesen's name was shouted by the voices of excited men. He hurried to the doorway, and there met messengers from Rameses, bearing torches and surrounded by many of his slaves and members of his household.

A captain stepped forward, and saluted him.

"I bear the commands of the mighty Pharaoh to my lord, the adon Martiesen, if he be alive; otherwise to the second in command," said the soldier.

"The commands of the ruler of Egypt are heeded wherever given," responded the adon. "Present them."

"My lord, there was no time for written commands, for the city and the court of Pharaoh are in sore distress. A flood of death has swept upon us, and I am told that you have not escaped it here. The firstborn in every household has been slain, and the land is in mourning. At midnight the destruction came upon us, and it was said to the king and his counselors that it was a punishment sent by the Hebrew God. Therefore a great cry arose in Rameses, that the Hebrews be driven out of the land, and the king sent us with swift rowers, to direct that no opposition be made by the forces at your command to the departure of these people from Zoan and from Goshen and from all the Hebrew settlements. They are a curse and a burden to Egypt, and the king declares that they must pass out of the land with all speed. His signet is here as a token that I speak his words truthfully."

The soldier stepped forward and displayed the ring, and Martiesen, looking at it, knew that the hour had come when Egypt and Israel would part.

"Let the rowers convey you to Zoan," said the adon, "and there show to Panas, lieutenant in charge of the command, the signet of the Pharaoh and this that I give to you, and speak the words of the king as you have done to me, saying to him that the words of the ruler of Egypt are also the words of the adon Martiesen."

The adon accompanied the messengers to the landing-place, and upon the way spoke with the captain of the visitation of the plague, the shadow of which rested on all of them at this moment.

"When it was said that the firstborn in each household had been slain, my lord, it was recalled that you were not only the firstborn, but also the only child of your illustrious father, and it was feared that the orders of the Pharaoh would of necessity be delivered to your lieutenant, Panas," said the captain, as they stood a moment at the landing. "The court will rejoice in your escape, and I doubt not that Meneptah will demand some explanation. If there is any message that you may wish to send to Rameses, my lord, I shall call for it on my return."

"There is none," replied the adon, "that would satisfy our ruler."

The captain hesitated a moment: "You will

pardon one long in the service of his country, my lord, for speaking plainly."

"You may speak freely what is in your heart," Martiesen assured him.

"It may come to the mind of the Pharaoh that Martiesen, the adon, was in league with those for whom he has long been known to entertain such deep sympathy, thus escaping the fate that has fallen so heavily upon all others."

The adon started visibly. "No, no, such suspicion could not arise," he said hurriedly. "Were it true, I should be a monster in whom the love of home and friends and kindred had turned to hate. My greatest enemy could not believe this of me."

"But, my lord, the circumstance is most peculiar, if, indeed, it shall prove that you alone, of all the firstborn of Egypt, shall have escaped."

With these words the captain entered the barge, and in a moment the swift craft darted out upon the Nile.

Thinking deeply upon what the soldier had said, Martiesen turned, and he was proceeding to the portico, when he met Elisheba on her way to the wharf. As she approached, the adon detained her gently.

"Elisheba, will you go hence with your people?"

"It is so ordered, Martiesen, by the mighty God Himself."

"Why did you risk so much, brave so much, to save me from death?"

"Because of my love for you," she answered, not concealing the truth.

"And yet you will not remain in Egypt as my bride?"

"It may not be," she replied, smiling sadly.

"Then why is it you have not left me to the fate of all the firstborn of Egypt?"

"My lord — "

"Nay, Elisheba, do not longer speak to me with formality. I am not your lord, your master, but the humble lover, pleading for your heart, your love."

"O Martiesen! You have my heart, you have my love, and they have been in your keeping ever since I saw you first in Zoan. Nor will absence, or distance, or time take them from you."

She paused a moment, and when more fully composed she continued: "When I was told of the sentence that had been pronounced of God against the Egyptians," she said slowly, "I knew that if the one I loved should be counted among the victims, I could not leave this land, and ever look upon one hour of happiness. But if I might save him from the fate that threatened, and bid him farewell in life and health, knowing that he remained in the place and land that were his by birth, then I could go forward with my people, and until my last day the song of love for Martiesen would arise from my heart. Even after many years I should picture that Martiesen's love for me had never grown cold, and that here beside the Nile still lived my lover."

The adon did not reply, but trembled with deep emotion.

"The day hastens," she said, turning towards the landing. "Farewell, my lord, my lover!"

"Farewell, Elisheba?" and he resisted her attempt to leave him.

"Yes, Martiesen, farewell. I must obey the commands."

"Of your heart?"

"Nay, but of my God."

He stood a moment looking into her eyes, deep and lustrous in the faint light of the coming morning. They did not waver, and he knew that her love, great as she had said, would not move her to change her resolution. Nor did he wish it, for his mind was made up.

"Then will I go with you, Elisheba," he said quietly.

"You must not, Martiesen. Think again of what you sacrifice, if you do this."

"My love for you is stronger than my love for treasure and power, Elisheba."

"But your country, your ancestral home, the tombs of your fathers!"

"My love for you is stronger than these ties, Elisheba."

"The Hebrews are wanderers from this day, and are going hence into the wilderness where want, and danger, and sorrows abound."

"My love and my care can lighten these burdens from your shoulders, Elisheba."

He gazed into her eyes, until the mantling blood crimsoned her cheeks.

"Elisheba, while I love you thus, can you bid me stay?"

"No, Martiesen, for your love is returned, and my heart forbids my tongue to frame that which I ought to say. Yet I would not see you take up the hardships that must come upon us who are commanded to go upon the search for a new land of promise, the borders of which we may not reach until the lapse of weary years. If you will lead me to the landing-place, and bid me go, I will carry

your love in my heart through all my life, knowing that he who gave it remains in the place that is
his to fill."

She regarded him sorrowfully for a long
moment.

"You cannot now leave here, Martiesen," she
said at length. "How is it that you say you will go
with my people when there is that to do here
which you cannot escape?"

"I have thought upon that, Elisheba. Is the way
known which the Hebrews will take?"

"To Moses only has God revealed the way."

"Then Bariet will act as my spy. After the
Hebrews have departed, he will return to me
here, bringing information that will enable me to
follow you. Two days from this I should be ready
to start. I have slaves to free and treasure to
divide among those who have been faithful
retainers in my house; but they must hear no
word of my intention to leave Egypt, lest the king
be informed and hold me a prisoner. The
Hebrews will of necessity move slowly, for with
the women and children, the aged and infirm,
and all their flocks and herds, their progress
cannot be rapid. It will not be difficult for two
men to overtake you."

He paused, for the mournful cry of those who

wailed for the dead came to their ears.

"But for your love and courage, Elisheba, I should be as one of those for whom they mourn."

"My lord, a fear comes to my heart, that it is out of gratitude for the little I have done that you are persuaded to surrender all that is yours to hold, receiving only my love in return."

"My loved one, did I not tell you long ago that when the Hebrews depart from Egypt, I should be at your side? It did not require this last proof to teach me your full worth. I knew it then, and every day this knowledge has grown, until it fills my soul and shuts out every other thought."

He put a square of cloth into her hands, woven of the finest linen and silver threads, and fringed with crimson. Embroidered in the center was a falcon, poised for flight, all a-glitter with the coloring of the living bird.

"It is my standard," he said, "and to it many men have rallied in battle against the foes of Egypt. Take this to Panas, and whenever the Hebrew hosts pause, night or day, let this float from the stave of a long spear, above the spot where you may rest. Then, when I come, it will guide me to your side, and from that moment our lives will run together."

He led her to the landing-place, where Bariet

was waiting with the boat, unloosed for instant departure. "Bariet," said the adon, "as you go to Zoan, Elisheba will explain what I would have you do. I bid you guard her until you find her father, and leave her by his side. On your return, you shall have full reward."

And then to the maiden, waiting there by his side: "Farewell, Elisheba, though my heart is heavy as the words are spoken. Ere your eyes turn for the last time upon an Egyptian scene, I shall be with you, and together we shall go forward in the path pointed out by the Hebrew God."

"Farewell, Martiesen, my lord, my lover, my king!"

And, standing there upon the step nearest the water, Martiesen watched the boat, until the form of Elisheba was swallowed up in the glory of the rising sun.

CHAPTER XXIV

THE EXODUS

A LONG, weary way it is over the hot fields of Egypt, eastward from Rameses, through the rough, narrow, almost verdureless mountain passes, to Pithom and Etham, and upon it slowly toiled forward six hundred thousand men, marching five abreast, and bearing upon their backs the heavy burdens that constituted their equipage. In two great divisions they marched, and between those two bodies were the women, the children, the aged and infirm, numbering four times the thousands of men in the ranks. Their lowing, wondering herds were with them, and added not a little to the picturesqueness of this strangest panorama ever witnessed by the eyes of man in any age.

A pastoral people, trained only to peaceful scenes, and not knowing the form of land lying beyond the horizon within which they were born; a people more than half barbarian, to whom in generations had not come the thought that any other condition awaited them; a superstitious people, who had absorbed many strange fantasies from those who held them in servility; an impetuous, passionate people, in whom obedience and control had only been invoked by fear; an obstinate, willful people, who often turned deaf ears to their appointed leaders. Yet league upon league they dragged wearily forward, led by one towering, silent, mighty man, not knowing in what direction, without knowledge of their destination, with scarcely any preparation for their sustenance.

Escaping from bondage? Yes, but through what door!

This only they knew of the way: that leading on before them stood a pillar of cloud by day, ever receding as they approached, and beckoning them on and on into the unknown wilderness. And when the night came, the cloud became a glowing light that illumed the way, and still led on.

Thus days and nights succeeded with little rest, but whenever the motley pilgrims paused, if only for one hour of rest from the weary march, the glistening standard of Martiesen floated above those who comprised the household of Darda. Elisheba never saw it raised except with hope, and never saw it furled except with sorrow; and yet she did not falter. When the order to march was given after a pause, she carried the fabric in her arms, and went forward with the belief that when next it were displayed, it would bring her lover to her side. But as the days and nights passed without tidings of Martiesen, there came to Elisheba the natural fear that when he reached the point where he must turn his back upon the Nile, he who had pledged his love to her, would find in that parting from home and country a bitterness which could not be borne. Nor could she blame him if he surrendered to the charm, and in the home of his ancestors kept his place as she had bidden him. There came to her no thought of resentment. In her heart his image would ever rise, and to it she would pay sweet homage through her life.

Southward they turned at Migdol and Pi-hahiroth, the bitter lakes, to which many ran to slake their thirst, only to find the waters laden with salt; and then on, over a flat, sandy, burning plain, to the sea.

On their last day's struggling journey toward

the sea, they learned that in their wake, with chariots and chosen warriors to man them, came the army of the Pharaoh.

In front of them, stopping all progress in that direction, stretched the wide, shallow arm of the Red Sea, a barrier across which they could not hope to pass. In the rear, and shielded only from their sight by the friendly pillar of cloud, their guide hitherto and now their protector, was the Egyptian host, bearing weapons of death, and led by the angry, eager king, who had in a measure recovered from the fear that had come upon him after the visit of death, and was now fired with a determination not to let the people escape who had so long been his slaves.

Thus encompassed, men looked into each other's faces in quest of hope; then turned with sinking hearts, and saw their wives and little ones and aged parents crouching in mute and piteous fear. A murmur went through the camp, faint at first, but swelling louder as it progressed, and they asked if there were no graves in Egypt, that they should be led away to die in the wilderness. Then men came and demanded of their leader why they had been brought forth, for it were better to have remained as servants of the Egyptians and have life, than to journey to this desolate place and here meet death.

But with never-faltering faith, scorning their murmurs and complaints, the mighty leader bade them cease their fears and look upon the salvation which would surely come this day. Then, standing there before them all, he stretched his hands over the waters, and in an instant the dull, heavy air became alive. From the east arose a gentle zephyr, which caught the standard of the adon, and sent it streaming from the lance-staff. The zephyr swelled into a breeze, and then into a strong and rushing wind, which piled the waters into waves, and the tumbling white caps leaped fast upon each other in their race for the open sea.

Night fell, and the people of Israel bent their heads to the ground, to escape the clouds of drifting sand which rolled along the tumultuous coast — all save one woman, who crouched against a willowy staff, and kept, as best she might, the emblem of her lover where it would show the way.

CHAPTER XXV

THE SEASON OF WATERS

"FATHER NILE is awakening. He comes again in his might to refresh his children!"

The cry of the couriers was taken up by the people along the shores, and found its way to homes in which the mourners had not ceased their lamentations, and were still crouching in fear.

"It is because the Hebrews have left us," they said to one another.

"Praise Osiris! Praise Isis! Yea, praise Osiris, for it is he who hath awakened Father Nile!"

So rang the shouts, and then chants of praise arose from lips which but a moment before had given utterance to sobs.

As Martiesen and Bariet, in light marching array and carrying knapsacks of supplies, stepped

from the portico of the adon's home, the tidings
that had been passed from mouth to mouth all
the weary leagues from distant Meroë came to
their ears. The adon paused, and with swelling
heart saw that the cry inspired hope in his people,
for its very echo summoned them to the river
bank, and they ran with waving arms and shouts
of joy. Lovingly he gazed upon the glistening
waters sweeping before him. "There is none so
fair, none so mighty, none so mysterious as the
Nile, and yet upon its bosom I may never after
this day be borne again. Ah, Father Nile, thou art
a wondrous god, and it is hard indeed to tear
oneself from thy side, though I go to follow one
who is thy master."

Bariet, who had remained with the Hebrew
hosts until he was well satisfied as to the general
direction they intended to pursue, had returned
to the villa two days before, to find that preparations were well advanced for the departure of his
master.

Almost at the hour of his return, private
advices of a most disturbing nature came to the
adon from Rameses. The suspicion, which the
Pharaoh's captain sent to command the Hebrews
to depart had expressed to the adon on the

morning following the destruction of the firstborn, had arisen in the court, and it was reported
that the ruler of Egypt might command the
presence of Martiesen and require of him an
explanation of how he had secured immunity
from the fate that had fallen with such crushing
weight upon all who were not of the Hebrew race.
When this was confided to Bariet by his master,
the devoted slave urged immediate flight, but the
adon would not listen. He was determined to
carry out the plans he had made. However,
preparations for the journey were soon
completed, and on this morning they were ready
for departure. Without farewells of any nature —
for only to an aged steward who was charged with
the execution of Martiesen's commissions had his
intentions been disclosed — the two men entered
the phaselus, and, each taking an oar, they shot
rapidly out into the stream, and turned westerly,
towards Rameses. For more than two hours they
toiled steadily, scarcely pausing to exchange
greetings with the crowds of rejoicing people
gathered upon the banks, shouting again and
again, as if they would never tire, the tidings that
had brought them new life — that the inundation
of waters was at hand.

Once, indeed, they paused. It was at a village where the ceremony of greeting to the river was already under way.

"It would be regarded as an insult, Bariet, did we not join them," said Martiesen. "We will not remain until the ceremony is concluded, but will at least show that we share their happiness by taking part for some time in the festival."

More than a score of boats soon put out from the wharf, following one in which were a priest and the several dignitaries of the community. Constantly the priest chanted praises to the gods, while those who accompanied him at intervals made offerings of various nature to the river itself. When at last the chant was concluded, a fanfare of musical instruments arose from the accompanying boats, and the people on shore shouted anew their praises to the god of the Nile, and, running to the river edge, danced gleefully in the shallow waters, or plunged boldly into them, and swam in playful circles far out from the shore.

The festival was at its height, when a low word spoken by Bariet caused Martiesen to turn his head in the direction toward which they had been proceeding. He saw approaching two of the smaller war galleys, bearing the royal insignia of the Pharaoh.

"Draw quickly in with the press of boats nearest the shore," said Martiesen, without betraying emotion. "This may be an expedition on its way to the Nome of the Prince, and we do not care to intercept it."

Bariet did as directed, and soon mingled with the revelers, who were so intent upon the sport in which they were engaged that they had failed to observe the approach of the galleys. However, some of the outlying boats discovered the coming of the royal craft, and speedily put out for the purpose of extending greetings, and securing whatever small coins and information the commander might be disposed to give. The clang of a gong caused the long oars to poise in mid-air, and showers of glistening drops fell from the immovable and rigid blades.

"Greetings, my brothers," said the commander, rising in the bow of the first galley. "Father Nile is awakening! The gods are good."

"Aye, the gods are good," responded the villagers, in chorus. "Praise Osiris, praise Isis! Yea, praise Osiris, for he is the greatest of all gods."

"He is indeed," replied the soldier, "for he has thwarted the designs of the Hebrews' God, and sends the mighty Nile to refresh our land."

"The brave men who have fought the battles of Meneptah, Wearer of two crowns, and Ruler of Lower and Upper Egypt, and Conqueror of all the nations of earth, are welcome," said the priest, whose boat had precedence, and was nearest the galleys. "Our festival is a humble and modest one, and would be graced by your presence."

"It may not be at this time, my brother, as we are charged to execute our orders without delay," apologized the officer.

"The errand must, indeed, be urgent," persisted the priest, "that it should call men from rejoicing and from praising the gods, upon a day when tidings come from Meroë that Father Nile is lifting up his mighty head at the command of Osiris."

The soldier hesitated. He knew well the widespread belief, that great danger attended any business or warlike venture attempted upon the day on which all the country rang with the message shouted by the couriers from that distant point at which the first sign of the coming inundation could be observed. Raising his voice, he shouted so loudly that all might hear him.

"Who amongst you does not mourn the death of the firstborn in his family?"

"Alas! none," replied the priest, and a wail arose from those who heard. "We were heavy with weeping until the joyous tidings came with the rising sun."

"And so it is, my brother, throughout all Egypt, save alone in one house. We are sent to bring before the Pharaoh him who escaped, that he may make explanation of conduct that gained for him alone the favor of the Hebrew God."

"Then speed, my brother, and may the gods aid you," answered the priest.

The gong sounded twice, and with the precision of a massive machine, the oars dipped in steady strokes, and the galleys swept majestically upon their way.

As soon as it was possible, the adon and his companion detached themselves from the party of villagers, and pursued their journey. They had been taken for fowlers, large numbers of whom sought the intersecting canals with the earliest news of the rising of the Nile, and made ready their snares for the first catch of birds.

Martiesen was preoccupied for a long time, and gave himself up to thought. It was repugnant to his proud spirit to quit his country with this imputation resting upon his name; but he realized that the hope was small indeed that he might purge himself from the charge made against him, even though he should proceed to Rameses and offer an explanation. The priests and magicians who had contended against the prophets from the start would demand his life, or, what was infinitely worse, his banishment to the mines, where death would be welcome every hour of the day or night. It was an absolute certainty that he was prejudged, and it was extremely doubtful whether any friend of influence in the royal court would have the courage to defend Martiesen's innocence. The utter hopelessness of any attempt at justification was so convincing that the adon made no objection when, soon after midday, Bariet changed their course toward the southern bank of the river, and their boat entered one of the larger canals, which led out across the plain, toward the eastern range of mountains. Once he turned, when they had entered the canal, and rising, gazed long and lovingly upon the Nile — then took the oar again, and went forward, no longer an adon of Egypt.

Scarcely pausing for refreshment, they toiled steadily through the long, hot afternoon, passing the length of many irrigating ditches and ponds, in which they found scarcely water enough to float their shallow craft. On those who assisted them through locks and dams, they bestowed coins, and with all they exchanged greetings, or rejoiced over the tidings that had so mysteriously spread before them, and which none tired of repeating — that the Season of Waters was at hand.

⌢⌢ⅢⅢ

CHAPTER XXVI

THROUGH THE SEA

THEY came at last to the point where the southern rim of the basin of the Nile stopped further progress of the canal, and the arid plain, almost destitute of verdure, stretched away toward the distant mountains. A few low, dark, mud-dried houses clustered about the head of the channel they had been following, and in front of them were ill-looking men, lowbrowed, shrinking women and children, who stared at Martiesen and his companion through thick strings of matted hair. It was not often that these people saw visitors from the vicinity of the main highway of Egypt, and those who did come were generally tax-gatherers, sent to exact the full limit of tribute, who did not spare the lash in exacting their commissions. Therefore, it was not strange that the men who landed from the phaselus were looked upon with suspicion, and treated with scant courtesy.

Martiesen approached the group, and employed the usual greeting announcing the coming of the inundation. For the first time during the day they had come upon a place so remote that the news they bore had not preceded them. He saw the light of joy come into their faces, and the dull, listless forms were in a moment electrified by the message that bore them the promise of life.

"Sayest so, master, sayest so in truth?" questioned several of the men, gathering about Martiesen.

"Aye, brothers, indeed it is true. Father Nile is stirring now in his bed, and soon will fill your canals and ditches."

Shouts of rejoicing and praise followed this assurance, and the desolate landscape itself appeared to take on a brighter tone and light up with warmer hues.

"We have little here, master," said the head man approaching Martiesen, "but we will hide nothing from you. Take freely such as you may find, only leave us seed and some little sustenance against the Season of Waters."

"We have come, my brother, to take nothing, but rather to give. I seek guides on the way towards Migdol, and must have them. For the service, I will give the village my boat and its equipment, silver to pay your tithes, and compensation to those who aid me."

The wondering villagers consulted together a few moments, and finally three came forward, who had been selected to act in the capacity of guides. Martiesen gave the head villager his cartouche, to prove legal possession of the phaselus, and a purse in which there was more treasure than the man had ever possessed in all his life.

Four hours of daylight remained when the party started out, and Martiesen was assured that they would reach the caravan route that led through the Migdol pass before nightfall. His guides proceeded rapidly, and though the country was rough and encumbered with stones, they soon left the Nile valley far behind. With each step hope grew stronger in Martiesen's breast, and he constantly urged the guides to greater speed, and secured it through the promise of larger reward. Frequently he made inquiry as to their progress, and when at last the villagers darted forward rapidly a few hundred yards and threw themselves down, exhausted, in the sand, Martiesen followed in anger, and demanded why they had paused.

"Look, master," said one of the guides, pointing before him, "what you seek, it is here."

Yes, it was there — the unmistakable evidence written there before him, that over this ground had passed a multitude of people — and somewhere on that road that led toward freedom for the mighty host that pursued the course had pressed the feet of Elisheba!

Martiesen could scarce restrain himself, or control his emotions. He dismissed his guides with a few words and liberal gifts, and taking some part of the luggage they had borne, he ran with the speed of a courier along the broad, beaten path that wound through the pass, glancing right and left over the ground, in the vain hope that he might discover some token of those whom he sought. In his eagerness he left his companion far in the rear, but at length Bariet overtook him, and begged that a more leisurely pace be followed. In time they approached the intersection of another pass, which opened upon

the plains some two leagues nearer Rameses than
the one which they traversed, and here they
paused out of sheer weariness.

Darkness was approaching when, after a brief
rest, they started up, but they had proceeded only
a few paces when Martiesen stopped as though
petrified, and stood gazing at the ground before
him. Bariet came to his side in alarm, and inquired if his master was ill. For reply, Martiesen
pointed to the roadway, but spoke no word.

"Chariots!" whispered the slave, as he bent to
scan in the gathering darkness the marks that
could not now be mistaken.

"Aye, chariots," replied Martiesen, gloomily.

"But, master, the Hebrews have neither
chariots nor chargers. Whence came these?"

"Look around you, Bariet," said Martiesen after
a few moments lost in thought. "Here we came
on the trail of the Hebrews through the pass that
leads back to Migdol. Here on the right enters
still another pass that leads out to the open plain
not many leagues from Rameses. Now, look close
upon what is written here before us. Do you not
see where the paths are joined, that the warlike
force has come upon the trail of the Hebrews
since they passed? The feet of the horses and

the wheels of the chariots have obliterated all traces left by those who are led by Moses."

Bariet gazed in mute alarm at what he now saw all too plainly, then, slowly turning to his master, in a tone of deepest apprehension asked:

"My lord, is it not the Pharaoh?"

"Aye, the Pharaoh!" replied Martiesen, with whitened lips. "Untaught by the lessons which have been sent him, the mighty lord of Egypt has summoned his hosts of warriors, and now leads them in the wake of those fleeing from his oppression, it may be to his complete overthrow, or it may be to the utter destruction of those whom he pursues."

"The Hebrews cannot withstand the chariots of the Pharaoh, my lord. They have no armed men."

"Of themselves they cannot withstand him, Bariet, as we who have fought with his armies well know. But great wonders have been wrought before our eyes, wonders not equaled by the gods, nor yet by the power of the Pharaoh. There may be held in reserve a final blow for those who have grown so proud and boastful of their power."

Night was now fallen, and Martiesen and his companion decided to proceed as rapidly as possible in the darkness, resting but an hour or two, and to take such course as should best commend itself when they approached the rear-guard of the army. They knew that the Egyptian host was a force of great mobility and would move rapidly. Martiesen, who was acquainted with the topography of the country toward which they were proceeding, realized that the Hebrews were entrapped. He explained to Bariet, that beyond the mountain pass lay a wide, sandy plain, and then the sea. The fear came to their minds that even at this hour the charioteers of the angry king might be awaiting the morning, and the signal to rush forth in dreadful carnage and massacre.

On and on they toiled through the night, and with the morning they came upon the almost level plain that stretched away before them in the burning sun. As far as they could see, there came to their vision trace of neither those whom they sought, nor those whom they feared to find; yet straight away before them led the broad road, stamped in the sand by the fleeing millions and their pursuing foes. Half the forenoon passed before they reached the spot where the Egyptians had camped the previous night. It was beside some wells in the midst of a grove of stunted trees that the camp had been pitched, and around them were all the evidences of a recent occupation. Indeed, some of the camp equipage lay in disorderly heaps, as though it had been cast down to remain but a few hours and be taken up again when the victorious army should return from the bloody errand upon which it was bent.

Yet they must not pause. They were lithe, active, hardened men, accustomed to feats requiring great endurance. Fatigue should not hold them back, for there, beckoning them on over the trembling sands, led the way. Hour after hour they ran, pausing only a few moments upon the slight elevations to scan the horizon or cast away some article of clothing or equipment grown burdensome. Each moment brought new evidence that they were gaining in the race, for the marks made by the chariot wheels were sharper and more distinct as league after league sped under their flying feet.

It was nearing sunset when Bariet, who was a few paces in advance, stopped suddenly as they came to the summit of one of the sand drifts, and pointed towards the south.

"See, my lord," he cried, "the Egyptians!"

Martiesen saw a cloud of dust toward which the Assyrian pointed, and well he knew its meaning. "True, Bariet; there ride the Pharaoh and his army. In an hour we shall come up with them, and by that time the darkness will have fallen. Then we shall learn the fate of our friends."

"I cannot believe, my lord, that the Egyptians have overtaken the Hebrews; for see, they are moving steadily forward. Which way lies the sea?"

"Here at the left, some distance away. We are approaching it at an angle. The Egyptians are not over three leagues from the shore."

"Then the Hebrews must be immediately in front of their pursuers."

"Yes, no doubt they have reached the water's edge, and by this time they must be in the gravest alarm over the situation in which they are placed."

In the gathering darkness Martiesen and Bariet drew close to the stragglers in the rear of the Egyptian camp. For the last half-hour they had been fighting their way in clouds of sand, which an unexpected wind lifted from the plain, and hurled against them with tremendous force. In the darkness and confusion they came upon a charioteer, whose steeds were rearing and plunging beyond his control, for the wheels of his chariot, clogged with sand, were firmly set upon the axle, and would not move.

"The gods have deserted me," he called in despair, as he saw the shadowy forms of Martiesen and his companion. "My chargers are possessed with evil spirits, and will not obey my voice."

"Where are those who should help you?" asked Martiesen, while Bariet ran to the heads of the horses, and attempted to quiet them.

"All is confusion in the storm which the accursed Hebrews have sent upon us," replied the soldier. "The slaves are in terror, and do nothing but wail; the drivers and their steeds are blinded by the sand; the chariot wheels cling to their axles, and many are broken off; the captains cannot keep their companies in order; Isis and Osiris have deserted us; all is confusion."

"Where are those whom you pursue?"

"We do not know, for strange lights and clouds have been before us, and we could see naught save the pathway where they trod the sand. Then the wind burst upon us, and with it came the night."

The soldier was shivering with fear. Bariet

assisted him in unharnessing his horses, and the poor beasts sank in terror upon the ground. As they listened, Martiesen and Bariet could hear, above the roaring wind, the appeals of men shouted to their gods, and the neighing of the frightened animals, now almost beyond control.

"We must avoid the Egyptian camp," said Martiesen. They had drawn aside. "I should be recognized by some of the captains, and be regarded as a spy. We will turn towards the sea, and perhaps we may be able to flank them."

Clasping hands, they faced eastward, and met the gale in all its fury. The sharp grains of sand were driven against them with a force that pricked the skin like needles. They bent low, and struggled on in the darkness, not knowing whether in the right direction, but keeping steadily against the wind. Hour after hour, slowly they fought their way, until they found the rounded pebbles of the shore beneath their feet.

"My lord," called Bariet into the ears of his master, "this is the place of the sea, but the water has disappeared."

The storm of sand was over now, for they were away from the dry plain from which the wind lifted it in clouds, but the gale continued unabated. Cautiously they proceeded down the sloping beach, but found under their feet only bunches of sea-grass and the shells and mussels.

"A way has been opened to deliver the Hebrews!" shouted the adon.

"The waters have been driven back by the wind, and here their God will lead them through to safety."

It was lighter now, for the dawn was breaking, and they turned toward the south, and ran with the wind upon the smooth sea-bed. Neither fatigue, nor thirst, nor hunger held them back, but on they sped, watching with anxious eyes for those who, they felt, must be near at hand.

A league they ran, and then Bariet stopped suddenly, and caught Martiesen by the shoulder.

"Look, master, the Hebrews!" He pointed to a long, dark, swaying line, and Martiesen knew that the people of Israel were marching fearlessly into the sea.

Soon he came up beside them, and running back along the column, he saw, still fluttering at the camping place, upon a higher portion of the shore, the white emblem of that rank which for all time he had laid down.

A shout from Panas, a word of quick surprise from Serah, a cry of wondrous joy from Elisheba, and Martiesen at long last reached the dark-eyed Hebrew maiden, whose faith had never wavered from the hour in which his promise was given.

William Walker Canfield
(1854-1937)

William W. Canfield was an accomplished writer,
a passionate and talented newspaper editor and
a highly-respected member of his community. He
wrote over fifty short stories and seven books,
including one book, *The Spotter*, which was one of
the six bestsellers of 1907, and his newspaper
career spanned over sixty years.

Born on July 6, 1854, in Ellicottville, NY,
William Canfield decided not to follow in his
father's footsteps as a farmer due to his great fear
of snakes. Instead, with his father's blessing, he
secured a three-year position as a printer's
apprentice. At the age of 20, Canfield began

work as a cub reporter for the *Buffalo Courier*. After several months, due to sickness, he left his job with the *Courier* and traveled throughout northwestern Pennsylvania and southwestern New York working various jobs for several different newspapers as he regained his health. In Randolph, NY, a group of locals convinced him to start his own newspaper, the *Randolph Courant*. After three years with the *Courant*, Canfield left and took a job with the postal service as chief clerk in Syracuse, NY. Responsible for 10,000 miles of postal lines, Canfield became acquainted with Mr. Bailey, the postmaster of Utica, NY, and more importantly, the editor of the *Utica Observer*, which later became the *Utica Observer-Dispatch*. Mr. Bailey convinced Canfield to take a position with his newspaper and, in 1889, Canfield became the city editor where he served for the next 24 years. It was during this time that he wrote his books. In 1913, upon the death of Mr. Bailey, Canfield became the editor, a position which he filled until his death at the age of 83. His last editorial was published on August 23, 1937, only five days before his death.

As an editor, his goal was to, "... try to put something in the paper every day that will be useful and helpful to somebody." Committed to justice, Canfield was well-known as a man who could never straddle an issue. Over his long career, Canfield had the distinction of writing editorials upon the deaths of 11 different Presidents of the United States. One of William Canfield's ten editorial rules was, "Never write or approve printing of any article I would be ashamed to read, or read before a mixed company of men and women, adults, boys and girls, in my own home."

Thank you to Mr. Jon K. Broadbooks, Editor of the Utica Observer-Dispatch, for permission to reprint the photograph of William W. Canfield from the front page of the August 29, 1937, edition of the Observer-Dispatch.

Thank you to the Oneida County Historical Society for their help in obtaining this biographical information.

LaVergne, TN USA
09 October 2009
160366LV00001B/18/A